The Telltale Lilac Bush

Dear Julie,

Hi! Isn't this a neat pen!
I bought it off of Mrs. Hayes in WV Studi
Thanks for letting me borrow your book in
here so I wouldn't get bored out of my mine
I like those black shoes you are wearing too.
— Cool ni-lighter isn't it!
But I have a major Problem! I know of

4 or 5 girls I like or could go with but I don
give me your advice
know who, here are the names

P.S. If you think
of any more girls
that you think I would
like let me know!

(Kinda I ← 3) Shannon Walker
don't know
if She would 4) Anna Cabanna
go with me or 5) Aren Sayre
not)

1) Jenifer Oldrage
2) Kelly Huey
3) Shannon Walker
4) Anna Cabanna
5) Aren Sayre

WRITE
BACK

Love,
Shaun
Imboden

The Telltale Lilac Bush

and Other West Virginia Ghost Tales

Ruth Ann Musick

THE UNIVERSITY PRESS OF KENTUCKY

ISBN: 0-8131-0136-0

Library of Congress Catalog Card number: 64-14000

Copyright © 1965 by The University Press of Kentucky

Scholarly publisher for the Commonwealth,
serving Bellarmine College, Berea College, Centre
College of Kentucky, Eastern Kentucky University,
The Filson Club, Georgetown College, Kentucky
Historical Society, Kentucky State University,
Morehead State University, Murray State University,
Northern Kentucky University, Transylvania University,
University of Kentucky, University of Louisville,
and Western Kentucky University.

Editorial and Sales Offices: Lexington, Kentucky 40506-0024

To THE MEMORY of my father, who told me my first ghost stories

Contents

Introduction   *page* xi

1. Jealous Rivals   1
    1. The Phantom Soldier
    2. The Mysterious Horseshoe
    3. The Domico Family
    4. What Price Love?
    5. The Legend of Boiling Springs
    6. Hunting Friends
    7. A Head and a Body

2. Wives Who Return   11
    8. The Telltale Lilac Bush
    9. The Chain
    10. The Face on the Wall
    11. Bill White's Wife
    12. Uncle Tom Howe
    13. The Tragedy at the Spring
    14. The Blue Boy Hotel

3. Ghostly Children   25
    15. The Little Rag Doll
    16. Help
    17. The Baby in the Fireplace
    18. Rapping on the Door
    19. The Boy and the Trumpet
    20. The Running Child

4. Murdered Kinsmen   34
    21. *The Glass Jug*
    22. *Chop Chop*
    23. *Rose Run*
    24. *The Brother and His Horse*
    25. *The Shadow on the Wall*

5. Omens of Death   40
    26. *The Gate*
    27. *Shiny Eyes*
    28. *The White Horse*
    29. *The White Stallion*
    30. *White Death*
    31. *A Ride with the Devil*

6. Deadly Visions   48
    32. *A Dream*
    33. *Grandfather's Clock*
    34. *Death Warning*
    35. *The Voice in the Night*
    36. *Vision in a Field*
    37. *Captain Copenhaver's Ghost*
    38. *Christmas Tree*

7. Headless Ghosts   57
    39. *Return of the Headless Man*
    40. *The Headless Rider*
    41. *The Headless Husband*
    42. *The Old Well*

8. Hidden Money   62
    43. *Footsteps on the Walk*
    44. *The Haunted House*
    45. *Aunt Betsy Barr and Her Dog*
    46. *The Ghost Girl*
    47. *Aunt Bett's Ghost*
    48. *Hickory Nuts*

9. Haunted Places   70
    49. *The Floating Coffin*

50. *The Old Burnt House*
51. *A Skeleton Hand*
52. *The Upstairs Bedroom*
53. *Anna Conrad*
54. *Wizard's Clipp*
55. *Vinegar Hill*
56. *The Living Corpse*
57. *Old Gopher*
58. *The Ghost of Gamble's Run*

10. Negro Slaves   87
    59. *The Tombstone*
    60. *How Kettle Run Was Named*
    61. *The Cruel Slave Master*
    62. *The Unusual Saddle*

11. Murdered Peddlers   93
    63. *A Ball of Fire*
    64. *The Murdered Merchant's Ghost*
    65. *Strange Noises*
    66. *The Tin Cup*

12. Mine Ghosts   103
    67. *Big John's Ghost*
    68. *The Pointing Finger*
    69. *The Old Horse*
    70. *Section South Main*
    71. *The Blue Flame*
    72. *Big Max*
    73. *The Ghost of Jeremy Walker*
    74. *Post Inspection*
    75. *The First Husband of Mrs. James*
    76. *Possessed*

13. Railroad Ghosts   120
    77. *The Body under the Train*
    78. *Boardtree Tunnel*
    79. *The Headless Man*
    80. *The Phantom Wreck*

14. Animals and Birds   126
     81.   *The Tortured Sparrow*
     82.   *The Canary*
     83.   *The Cat*
     84.   *The Bench-Legged Dog*
     85.   *The White Wolf*
     86.   *The Phantom Dog*
     87.   *The Old Sow*
     88.   *The Junkman's Horse*
     89.   *Jack*
     90.   *The Strange Chicken*
     91.   *A Loyal Dog*

15. Weird Creatures   144
     92.   *The White Thing*
     93.   *The Strange Creature*
     94.   *Shortcut*
     95.   *The White Figure*

16. Immigrant Ghosts   150
     96.   *Seven Bones*
     97.   *The Corpse That Wouldn't Stay Buried*
     98.   *Draga's Return*
     99.   *The Old Crossroads*
     100. *Footprints in the Snow*

Notes   163

Bibliography   187

Introduction

A NYONE WHO has ever lived in West Virginia, or even traveled through the state, can easily see what an ideal place it would be for ghosts. It is an unending sequence of hills and valleys, with a backdrop of other mountains in the distance. Over all these mountains and valleys is a wilderness of shrubbery and trees so that genuinely lonesome places exist in almost all sections of the state. Hundreds or even thousands of ghosts could gather nightly on West Virginia's hills or sigh from the treetops, and few living souls would know the difference.

But West Virginia has more than a ghostly setting. As everyone knows, a ghost presupposes a murder, or at least an unusual death, and West Virginia has had no lack of either. The Mountain State can boast of a long list of such violent deaths throughout the years. Probably trouble with Indians, the Civil War, and mine accidents have contributed more generously toward ghost origins than any other factors, but cruel slave owners, the killers of wandering peddlers, and other murderers have helped too. It is altogether possible that one of my distant relatives, "Devil" Anse Hatfield, added to the number of West Virginia's ghosts.

And yet, in spite of the evident hard circumstances under which most of these unfortunate creatures died, West Virginia's ghosts, as a whole, do not come back for revenge.

It may be that many of them come back in a kind of nostalgia—to get another look at the hills. Even the victim of a scythe murder, over a hundred years ago, did not come back in malice. The poor thing evidently preferred West Virginia to wherever he was—and particularly wanted to locate his head, which had been separated from his body in death. Ghosts do not like such separations, but most of them are polite about it and, headless or otherwise, are far less hostile than people realize. In speaking of New York ghosts, Louis C. Jones says "far, far more come back with kindly purposes in mind—than come back in anger," and West Virginians are much the same. Perhaps the tales represented here may not bear this out very well, but my entire collection of ghosts will.

Since the early 1950s, a great deal of research has been completed on the folktale, including ghost stories. Ernest Baughman's Ph.D. dissertation, "A Comparative Study of the Folktales of England and North America," devotes 128 pages to Motif E with the addition of numerous motifs concerning the dead. Stith Thompson's *Motif-Index of Folk Literature* has been revised and enlarged to include much of the scholarship of the last thirty years. In the revision there are thirteen additional pages on Motif E. Also a number of ghost stories, or collections containing ghost tales, with comments and references, have come out within the last ten years.

Prior to 1950, various scholarly articles on ghosts had been published, including a study of "The Vanishing Hitchhiker," but the great surge of scholarly work on motif indexes (barring Stith Thompson's earlier six-volume edition), especially motifs concerning ghosts and the dead, has been made available only since 1950. Consequently, although comparatively few ghost tales could be identified some fifteen years ago, now almost all of them can be classified under one or more motifs.

However, even though they are a form of the folktale, and a very early form, comparatively few ghost stories can be identified as Tale Types. In the hundred tales represented here, only one, "Seven Bones," can be so identified. It is Tale Type 365, "The Dead Bridegroom Carries Off His Bride."

A selection of one hundred ghost stories could hardly give a complete picture of West Virginia's people. However, I think these tales do suggest something of their lives, oral culture, and beliefs. One may also read into this collection, as into any collection of folklore, something of the history of the state—even before 1863.

When I started to collect West Virginia folk material in the fall of 1946, it never occurred to me that any possible ghost story collection might be grouped to form a historical pattern. Now when I look over some of the classifications —"Negro Slaves," "Railroad Ghosts," "Animals and Birds," "Headless Ghosts," "Omens of Death," "Mine Ghosts," "Immigrant Ghosts,"—and think of the stories and beliefs involved, it seems to me that such tales could be grouped to represent a history of not only West Virginia, but almost any other state, and possibly even the United States.

Until recently, I had no idea that the ghost stories of a people might reflect their inner lives—their beliefs, fears, and hopes. Now, I think they may. For example, I understand when Negro workers were brought here from Alabama in the early 1900s to replace striking miners, the men had a terrible fear of the mines. Some of this fear may still exist, as shown in "Big Max." The beliefs of respective countries are also illustrated in "Possessed" (Italian), "Big John's Ghost" (Welsh), and "The Old Horse" (Hungarian), although all of these tales are supposed to have happened within ten miles of Fairmont. I have not found that the younger people, especially those whose parents or grandparents grew up in Europe, scoff at their older relatives' experiences or beliefs.

Perhaps a combination of circumstances has given West Virginia a plenitude of ghost stories. Its isolated hills and little-traveled roads were suitable scenes for deeds of violence. Even in the late 1700s, when unprotected settlements were being massacred by Indians or white renegades, the victims in western Virginia may have outnumbered other such sections because of the remoteness of the districts. Also, the dark wilderness itself may have given rise to supernatural beliefs.

These fatalities seem to have continued through the years, even in matters of the growth and development of the state. Railroads, road building, the construction of tunnels and bridges, all took heavier tolls in lives than usual, since the whole section was a mass of mountains. (In recent years there have been a large number of highway deaths for the same reason, although, barring "the hitchhiking girl" tales, of which all states have a number, few ghosts have been reported from them.)

The mines also have brought about a large number of ghost stories, possibly because of the backgrounds of the miners. Those who came from European and Asian countries could not, in most cases, understand or speak a word of English when they first arrived. It was natural that they would keep alive their native beliefs in the supernatural, shut off to themselves at first by the barriers of language, with the men spending most of their waking hours in semi-darkness. Negroes who came up from the South had their fears too, especially in the dark-of-the-mine, and particularly after the death of a fellow worker. In addition, the miners as a group had certain beliefs and superstitions, and no doubt added new ones after each fatal accident.

Sometimes such accidents would kill only one person—sometimes many. Unfortunately, accidents still occur and probably always will as long as there are mines, in spite of all precautions and engineering progress, but there is comparative safety now. In the early days the miners were in constant fear of slate falls and explosions. These mine accidents have probably taken more lives than any other single factor in the state, including the Civil War—possibly any three other factors. The Monongah explosion, on December 6, 1907, with 361 known dead, was one of the worst accidents in the United States, but there have been others, before and since—many others—but the worst ones came in the early days.

The early miners seem particularly pathetic to me; before the unions provided adequate wages, they were risking their lives every day for almost nothing—twelve cents a day, in some cases. And, once they were here, there was almost nothing they could do to escape, because they soon became hopelessly indebted to the company stores. The amazing thing to me is that, of all the ghosts of unfortunate miners, almost none of them come back in malice. Most of them seem to return to help the living, or because they just cannot stay away. These early-day miners must have been a particularly gentle and forgiving lot—but so were most of the other victims.

None of the stories here were told to entertain, or frighten, or to hold anyone in suspense. Almost all of them were told or written down by someone who believed he or the teller had had a supernatural experience. Even the legends that have been brought over from other lands are believed by the older taletellers to have actually happened to someone.

I have tried to set down these stories essentially as I received them. I have made certain minor changes, however, being always, I hope, careful not to violate the integrity of the story. Repetitious material and extraneous matter, for example, have been deleted entirely, and explanatory material, which was often introduced at the beginning of stories or was inserted to clear up a technical point, as in some of the mining stories, has been placed in the notes. Ambiguous sections I have tried to revise so that the flow of narrative runs as smoothly as possible. Since a number of the stories were reported to me by my students, who had heard them originally from relatives or neighbors, such minor changes as I have made serve not to violate the essential elements but rather to render them clearer and more distinct.

Sometimes people ask, "Where did you get all your ghost stories, and how?" Ghost story collecting is much like other folklore collecting. In addition to the method everyone uses—following up leads with a tape machine—my collection stems from three main sources: (1) my students at Fairmont College, (2) my weekly folklore column, which I wrote for six years, and (3) the little magazine, *West Virginia Folklore*, which I have edited since 1951. Also, since ghost stories have had a strong appeal for me since early childhood, it may be that I am unconsciously on the lookout for them at all times.

Although I have received many tales in response to my column, and as editor of the folklore booklet, my chief source of ghost tales has been my students. I realize there is a certain loss of both personal contact with the original teller and authenticity of wording when stories are retold by students, but as Louis C. Jones points out from his New York student material, it has its advantages too. It seems unlikely that one collector, working alone with a tape machine, could do as much as several hundred students, working for the collector through relatives and neighbors. And, as he states further, elderly people will often hesitate to make known to a stranger what they might willingly tell a younger relative or friend.

In any case, my students and I have rounded up hundreds of ghost stories—probably about a thousand in all, now—with little duplication. Most of the tales in this book come from the northern or central part of the state—only two from the southern border—and this probably holds for my entire collection. Geographically speaking, an ideal representation would be to have tales from every county, and since Fairmont College has students from all parts of the state, one might hope that this would be the case. So far, it is not. Fewer than half of the fifty-five counties are represented in this book.

In selecting and arranging these particular stories, I'm afraid I used no scholarly scheme whatever. I simply liked the tales myself and thought that most of them represented some phase of ghosthood rather vividly. In regard to the divisions used, since many of the stories fall under several classifications, a number of arrangements could have been made. However, the divisions used seem to follow a logical sequence, and the tales included under each of them seem appropriately placed.

For anyone interested, notes about the contributors, references to motif index numbers, and comparisons to similar stories in other collections are given at the end of the book.

Acknowledgments

SOME OF THE stories in this collection were previously published in *Midwest Folklore*, in *West Virginia Folklore*, in my weekly column, "The Old Folks Say," in the Fairmont *Times-West Virginian* from 1948 to 1954, and in my little book, *Ballads, Folk Songs and Folk Tales From West Virginia*, published by the West Virginia University Library, 1960. I wish to thank the publishers involved for permission to use the material again.

Also, I wish to thank all the contributors of stories, since without the stories there would have been no book. I particularly want to thank my students at Fairmont State College, especially those in my folk literature and freshman composition classes, for their help in gathering many of these stories and making them known to me. A large proportion of the stories here are theirs.

In addition, I would like to thank Dr. Herbert Halpert

of the Memorial University of Newfoundland for his kindness and generosity of time in suggesting helpful books for
examination in the project and Mrs. Elinor Watson Carroll
for her helpfulness in giving information about mining
terms and mines.

The full-page illustrations by Archie L. Musick of
Colorado Springs, Colorado, help immeasurably to convey
the authentic ghostly quality of these tales, and I am
grateful to him quite beyond a sister's duty.

Fairmont, July, 1964.   RAM

xviii

1   Jealous Rivals

Aʟᴛʜᴏᴜɢʜ I ʜᴀᴠᴇ included only seven fairly short tales in this section, I have a number of love-triangle ghosts. As I think over the tales I have, and the ones I know about, there seem to be far more situations where two men fall in love with the same woman than where the roles are reversed. Since the love triangle as found here always involves a slight or an injustice, there usually is an element of malevolence in the ghosts of these tales, and they end tragically. Literary examples of triangle situations rarely contain ghosts, and they favor the situation where two women love one man. Perhaps the latter situation allows for greater subtlety whereas the former is better suited to the more straightforward action of the folktale.

1. The Phantom Soldier

DURING WORLD WAR I, a young soldier from West Virginia was engaged to be married to a beautiful young girl, but was called into the army sooner than he had expected. He was sent to Germany. After he had gone, his older brother persuaded the girl that the soldier had not loved her after all, and married her himself.

On Christmas Eve, the soldier returned unexpectedly. A full moon lighted the sky, but the house on the hill, surrounded by pines, where his brother lived, seemed dark. The soldier knocked, and his older brother let him in, though he was obviously not pleased to see him. The wife was upstairs.

The two brothers talked for a few minutes. The older brother admitted that he had married the girl for her money and position, and added that, if the other interfered, he would not hesitate to kill him. The soldier left, but returned in a short while with a revolver and shot his older brother. He then left the house as quietly as he had come.

The young wife, hearing the shot, rushed downstairs to find her husband dying on the floor. He told her what had happened. Though the police, after she called them, made a thorough search, they could find no trace of the soldier.

On Christmas day a telegram arrived, addressed to her husband. It announced that his brother had been killed in action on December twenty-first.

2. The Mysterious Horseshoe

IN THE HAMLET of Tattletown there lived two lovely young women, Mary Angle and Rachel Hodge. They were both courted by James K. Henry. James Henry had a hard time deciding which one to marry, but he finally chose Mary Angle, and in January he and Mary were married.

Some thirteen months later, Mary died in childbirth, and James Henry sorrowfully erected a marker on her grave.

Three years later James Henry married the other girl, Rachel Hodge. Within a week after the marriage a mysterious shape appeared on Mary's tombstone. It looked like a horseshoe.

Shortly after the appearance of the strange horseshoe mark, James Henry went to his barn to do some chores and was kicked to death by Mary's pet riding mare.

There are those who say that at night the horseshoe on the tombstone glows and that there has appeared within its border the outline of two female figures apparently quarreling. What causes this no one knows, but the horseshoe mark, now eaten through the stone, still remains to this day.

3. *The Domico Family*

THE DOMICOS were a young married couple who came to Grant Town from Osage about 1932. Mr. Domico was a very hard worker and got along well with all the people in town. Mrs. Domico was a very beautiful woman about twenty-five years old.

Mr. Domico worked under a boss by the name of McCaulla. Mr. McCaulla was an older man whose wife had died and left him with six children to bring up. He fell in love with Mrs. Domico and came to visit her and her husband quite frequently. The Domicos considered him a very close friend and got along well with him. Mr. McCaulla moved into the house next door and brought the Domicos many fine gifts. He spent all his time over there talking with them.

One day McCaulla took Mr. Domico down into the mine and had him go to work in the blasting section. When lunchtime came, he asked Mr. Domico to go and check the charges. While Domico was doing this, one of the charges went off and he was killed.

About a year-and-a-half later, McCaulla married Mrs. Domico.

They were getting along fine until one day he went to work and saw Mr. Domico appear from the section where he had been killed. Domico asked why he had killed him. Every day, at noon, he would appear and ask the same question.

This went on for over two months, until one day McCaulla's body was found in the mine. He had committed suicide and left a note explaining the way he had killed Domico.

When she heard of this second death and how her first husband had been murdered, Mrs. McCaulla lost her mind and had to be taken away. Some of the McCaulla relatives from Pennsylvania came and took the children.

4. *What Price Love?*

MANY YEARS AGO in Freeland's Hollow, near Mannington, a tragedy occurred. Two young men, George Gump and Willie Jones, loved Helen Morgan, the prettiest girl in the community, and were bitter rivals. Each one tried to outdo the other. One would escort her to the spelling bees, while the other would take her to the church sings.

Young Helen, like all women, greatly enjoyed all this attention, and tried to keep both suitors dangling. Finally Willie Jones said she had to choose between them, so Helen agreed to marry him, and did. On the day of the wedding, George Gump made a vow that he would get even with his rival.

Six months passed happily, and Willie Jones, learning that he was to become a father, decided that he would buy his wife some new dress material on his next trip into town.

After he had finished his dealings with the stores, Willie stopped at a saloon, and it was almost midnight when he left town. On the way home, with his wagon full of supplies and with the dress material for his wife, he was attacked from behind and his head cut from his body.

To this day the murderer has not been found, and neither has George Gump. But, if you will go to Freeland's Hollow at midnight, when the moon is full, you will see a headless man riding in a spring wagon, with a bolt of calico hanging over the side.

5. *The Legend of Boiling Springs*

ABOUT TWENTY MILES east of Parkersburg, on U.S. 50, there is an old dirt road. About fourteen miles out that road there is a huge and very dilapidated old hotel. Many years ago, this hotel was one of the most popular resorts in West Virginia.

It was called Boiling Springs and was famous for its healthful mineral and sulfur springs. People from all over the eastern part of the United States came there. Suddenly, though, the resort began to lose popularity. Within a year it was closed up and completely abandoned, and no one has stayed there since.

No one knows, for sure, why this beautiful resort suddenly became deserted and unknown, but there is a story that might explain it.

Once there was a man staying at the hotel by the name of Grayson. He fell in love with a very lovely lady who was also staying there. Her name was Pearson. Another man named Miller, who was staying there, also fell in love with Miss Pearson.

One day Mr. Grayson saw Mr. Miller with Miss Pearson, and it made him very jealous. A few days later the two men got into a heated argument over the woman. The argument soon developed into a fight and the men fought so fiercely that they did not notice how close they were to the edge of the cliff which was in front of the hotel. They both fell over the cliff, and both died about an hour later. Miss Pearson, who actually loved Mr. Miller, was so grieved over the death of her lover that she killed herself by leaping from the cliff.

Soon the resort began to lose business. People began to hear weird noises in the hotel at night. Within a year no one would go near the place, because it was believed to be haunted.

6. *Hunting Friends*

Two young men had a lodge not far from Newburg where they would spend a few days together every year during the deer season.

They were very good friends, but they both fell in love with and courted the same girl. Finally she decided to marry one of them, Tom Ellis. At that, Jack Clayton, the other man, became jealous and bitter and ended what could have been a lifelong friendship. However, several months after the marriage, Mrs. Ellis prompted Clayton to visit them and resume his friendship with her husband.

Everything worked out fine—and just in time for the next hunting season. The two men, arm in arm, went off together to their old lodge. A few days later, Clayton came out of the woods alone. He said his friend had got lost. A search party went out, but didn't find any trace of Tom Ellis. The State Police thought there was something odd about the whole thing—in view of Clayton's earlier bitterness—but they could not prove anything, so the case was dismissed.

The following season Clayton went back to his camp with a new hunting partner. It had been a long trip, and so the first night there, the new man went to bed early. He was jolted awake by Clayton's screaming voice, saying, "Don't do it, Tom! Please don't do it. . . ."

Clayton's new hunting partner turned the light on and found Clayton sprawled on the floor, a hunting knife stuck in his heart, his face a mask of fright.

The following spring, police found Ellis' body buried not far from camp, with Clayton's hunting knife deep in his heart.

There has never been a definite answer to this case. The people from Preston County let you solve the murder of Jack Clayton to suit yourself.

7. *A Head and a Body*

IN AN OLD homestead near Mt. Harmony, one hundred and fifty years ago, lived a beautiful young woman named Mary Meadows. Every man for miles around wanted her for his wife, but she only cared for Tom Dixon, who, like herself, was young and handsome.

The wedding day was set, the big cabin was made ready, and the marriage took place. The young couple seemed to be ideally happy.

Some of Mary's many admirers were very disappointed over her choice of Tom Dixon. One man especially seemed broken-hearted. His name was Jack Wilson. He was an odd person who never forgot anyone that got in his way.

As the months passed, he got worse. He wouldn't talk to anyone, was always in the woods, and people saw less and less of him. Soon he was a type of wild man—bearded

and dirty, with clothes in rags, and eyes that had the look of a maniac.

While in Fairmont one day, Wilson saw the young wife alone and started at once to run toward the river and the ferry to take him across to Palatine and the road for Mt. Harmony. He ran all the way to Dixon's farm and then went into the woods nearby and got a scythe that he had placed there long before.

Like some wild animal, he crept up on Dixon, who was hoeing corn in his big cornfield. However, Tom's dog saw him and started to bark. Tom looked around just in time to see the wild-looking madman coming at him with a scythe. He started to run for the house, with Wilson close behind him. He had got as far as the well, when he tripped and, before he could get up, Wilson was upon him.

Now he had to fight for his life, and some fight it was, but he finally took the scythe and with one big swing cut off Wilson's head, which rolled into the well. Horrified at what had happened, he carried the body deep into the woods and hid it under the brush. He never said anything to his wife about the fight, and even killed a young pig and threw it into the well to keep anyone from using the water.

Two weeks passed. No one missed Wilson much because of his queer ways, and soon he was forgotten, or was believed to have left the neighborhood. However, he was anything but gone, and soon everyone was to know of him in a different way. Without any warning, Tom Dixon sold the farm and took his wife, who in the two weeks seemed to have aged twenty years, and moved to the Far West, never to be heard from again.

The new owner of the farm was a very good man by the name of Salters, who soon moved. This was the story he told.

Every night at 8:30, when the moon was full, he would hear a deep voice call out, "Where is my head?"

From down in the abandoned well, an answer would come, "Down here in the well."

Then the deep voice would say, "Where? I can't find the well."

Then after a short pause the voice would start all over and would be repeated over and over all night long, until the full moon would disappear the next morning.

This went on for years. Nobody would live in the house any length of time, and the farm was soon reclaimed by the woods.

2   Wives Who Return

Most ghost wives were in life mistreated, sometimes murdered, women, and their return is usually prompted by a desire to revenge themselves upon their former spouses. Two of the stories here, as well as others included in different sections, have examples of this kind of ghost. A third story is more a reenactment, as though the wife were conscious that she had in a way deserved punishment and she is merely repeating the circumstances of her death. Another story contains a kindly ghost; although the woman suffered to the point of ultimate despair, yet her manifestation guides her husband to safety and is responsible for his reform.

West Virginia's most publicized wife murderer, Harry Powers, who married women and killed them for their money, seems, however, to have brought forth comparatively few ghosts. Although there have been strange noises reported from his farm, Quiet Dell, I have received only four accounts of actual ghosts there, so far.

8. *The Telltale Lilac Bush*

AN OLD MAN and woman once lived by themselves along the Tygart Valley River. There had been trouble between them for many years. Few people visited them, and it was not immediately noticed that the wife had unaccountably disappeared. People suspected that the old man had killed her, but her body could not be found, and the question was dropped.

The old man lived a gay life after his wife's disappearance, until one night when a group of young men were sitting on his porch, talking of all the parties which the old man was giving. While they were talking, a large lilac bush growing nearby began beating on the windowpane and beckoning towards them as though it were trying to tell them something. No one would have thought anything of this if the wind had been blowing. But there was no wind—not even a small breeze.

Paying no attention to the old man's protests, the young men dug up the lilac bush. They were stunned when the roots were found to be growing from the palm of a woman's hand.

The old man screamed and ran down the hill towards the river, never to be seen again.

9. *The Chain*

EZRA GORDON was a hard-working carpenter, slightly eccentric, thrifty, and religious. Until his recent marriage to Sarah Garlow, he had seemed a confirmed bachelor. There

was considerable gossip about the marriage, and it was generally agreed that Sarah had married Ezra for his money.

Ezra built a house for his bride on five acres of ground he had owned for several years. All went well for a few months, but Sarah soon tired of the house, and living in the country irked her.

About that time oil companies began extensive drilling operations in the area and Brooksville became their headquarters. It rapidly changed from a sleepy village into a boomtown, with all the evils of fast growth and excess money.

The change had little effect upon Ezra Gordon. His services were always in demand and he had all the work he could handle. Such was not the case with Sarah. The gay life of the town had a special lure for her, and she made frequent trips, often returning home late at night. It was whispered that she had been seen in the company of other men, so it came as no surprise when Ezra reported that Sarah had run off with an oilfield supply salesman. Ezra then quickly settled his business, sold his house to Joe and Mary Blake, withdrew his money from the bank, and disappeared, leaving all who knew him feeling sorry for him.

Joe and Mary Blake felt sorry for him too, but their sorrow was overshadowed by their pleasure in acquiring his house. They had bought it at a bargain price, and it was just what they wanted. The day they moved in, they worked all day long setting up furniture, cleaning, polishing, and making plans.

Sleep came quickly that first night, since they were tired and worn out from moving. At about midnight, however, they were awakened by the sound of a dragging chain, but when Joe went to see what it was, he found nothing at all, although he looked everywhere.

The following night, the sound was repeated. At midnight, the clock struck twelve clear, deliberate notes. Mary

14

awakened. The clock had been a gift from her family. But now, she thought, it seemed to have a peculiar sound, louder than she remembered it. Her thoughts were interrupted by a noise. A clanking sound like a chain being dragged outside the bedroom door caused her to scream, "Joe! Joe!"

When Mary told him the noise had seemed to go downstairs, Joe ran down to investigate. He wasn't sure whether he opened the door or whether it came open by itself. One thing was sure, he had heard a clanking sound like a chain being dragged, but it was dark and he couldn't see anything.

The third night Joe and Mary climbed the stairs with apprehension. Sleep did not come this night. It was pitch dark outside. The low rumble of distant thunder warned of an approaching storm. A jagged bolt of lightning lit up the room. Together they glanced at the clock. It was five minutes before twelve.

Slowly the clock ticked. In the stillness of the room, each sound seemed deafening. Another bolt of lightning lit the entire room. One minute before midnight now.

The clock struck. Slowly, deliberately, the notes sounded one through twelve. At the precise moment the twelfth note ended, a dragging, clinking sound was heard outside in the hall. It seemed to come from a bedroom into the hall. Slowly it passed their door and clanked down the stairs. It seemed to drag along the porch and then drop to the ground. They heard it clink as it touched the stepping stones in the yard.

When Joe and Mary went downstairs, the front door stood open. Joe gazed intently into the darkness. Another flash of lightning streaked downward. The house trembled from the peal of thunder that followed. Then came the rain.

Joe and Mary quickly withdrew to the kitchen. There they huddled together, too upset to sleep, and they could do nothing more until the storm subsided.

15

With the gray light of dawn, the rain stopped. Joe went upstairs. He carefully examined the rooms and the stairs, but found nothing. His search then led to the porch, his wife at his side.

"Look, Joe," said Mary, pointing to a corner of the garden.

Joe's gaze fell upon a sunken depression in the ground. He glanced at Mary. They crossed the wet grass to the garden and examined the depression. It was about five feet long and no water stood in it. Joe got a spade. The soft, wet earth came out in huge clumps. In a few minutes his search was ended. There in a corner of their newly acquired garden lay the body of Sarah Gordon in a shallow grave. Her skull had been crushed by a heavy blow from a hammer or hatchet, and locked to her leg was a chain with which her husband had tried to keep her at home.

Joe and Mary sold the house at a much lower price than they paid for it. Several people tried to live in it, but they were unable to do so. They were all disturbed by the sound of clinking, dragging chains, pulled by the ghost of Sarah Gordon as it made its way from her room to her shallow grave in the garden. Uninhabited by mortals, the house became weatherbeaten, and it was eventually torn down to make way for the expanding town that had been the undoing of Sarah Gordon.

10. The Face on the Wall

IN MARCH, 1927, after five years of service with the railroad, Nick Yelchick was laid off. Unable to find a job, Nick decided to forget his troubles with a bottle. When he came home drunk, he would beat his wife and tear up the house. This went on for several months.

Finally, Nick was given a job in the mines. On Friday, after he had been working for five days, Nick asked his buddy at lunch to punch his timecard after work so he could go to the liquor store before it closed.

As soon as Nick finished his lunch, he decided to have a look around some of the worked-out sections of the mine. Before he realized it, he was lost. The more he tried to get back to the main line, the deeper he went. He walked for four hours before he realized that nobody was going to be looking for him because his timecard would be punched out, and there would be no way of knowing that he was still in the mine. His wife would think that he had gone on one of his weekend drunks.

About ten hours later his light burned out. Now he was really in trouble. He stumbled around for about two hours longer; then, too tired to take another step, he sat down and fell asleep. While he was sleeping, he dreamed he saw his wife's face on the wall of the mine, and she kept saying, "Follow me." This frightened him so much that he woke up. Just as in the dream, he saw his wife's face on the wall, so he started in the direction of the face. As soon as he got near it, another one would appear farther away. This went on for about two hours until finally he found himself on the main line. Now he was safe.

When he got out of the mine, the night watchman said, "Your wife was down here yesterday, looking for you, but we told her you'd gone home."

When Nick got home, he found his wife had killed herself. In a note she said, "I thought you would stop drinking when you got this job, but now I know different."

After that, Nick became a model citizen of Grant Town and was until his death in 1947.

11. Bill White's Wife

SOME YEARS AGO, during the oil and gas boom in Wetzel County, there lived in Rock Camp a family called White.

Mrs. White was a hard-working woman who did most of the work on the farm. Her husband Bill took odd jobs as a teamster, did a lot of horse trading, and was often away from home. Supposedly he had affairs with other women, and he quarreled with his wife and sometimes beat her over them. But she did not complain and refused to leave Bill, even though some of her children wanted her to come and live with them.

One summer Mrs. White took the fever and died. In a short while, Bill remarried. It was not long afterward that stories began to go around about strange things happening on the White farm. Two oilwell workers claimed they saw the dead Mrs. White around the engine house of a well they were drilling on the farm. The family, too, told stories. The ghost was seen making trips from the house to the springhouse. One night there was a sound like a lot of gravel being dumped on the roof, and on several evenings they could hear someone poking the fire in the cookstove and rattling the pots and pans. When they went to see what it was, they could hear someone moving through the door into the darkness outside. Other people reported hearing the sound of milking from the barn which stood close to the road; they also could find nothing when they looked into the barn. After these things had been going on for a while, a daughter, who had lived on at the farm after her mother's death, sold out her interest in the farm and moved out.

Finally, one evening as Bill was coming in from the fields and walking under the apple tree in the back yard, his dead wife seemed to come right up to him and say, "Bill, here is where you knocked me down with a chair."

Things began to go badly for Bill White and his second wife. Their cattle got sick, the horses both died, and the new Mrs. White became sickly. Finally they sold the farm and moved away. And that seemed to be the end of Mrs. White's ghost.

12. Uncle Tom Howe

IN THE SMALL coal-mining town of Copen lived a man by the name of Uncle Tom Howe and his wife. Uncle Tom made his living by farming. Both he and his wife were hard-working people, and when they started a job they didn't stop for rest until it was finished.

It was autumn and the leaves on the trees had just begun to turn brown. Uncle Tom Howe decided it was time to cut his large crop of wheat. Wheat was cut in this part of the country by harvesters, who came around to each farm with mowing machines. After several days the harvesters finally came, and on this day, Uncle Tom's wife was very sick. The men were working in the fields when Tom heard his wife call for him. He continued to work, but after she had called several more times, he went to see what was wrong.

She was in bed, crying with anger, when Tom came in. She asked him to please go and find a doctor, but Tom only shook his head. He said that the wheat had to be cut that day, and walked back to the fields. After the work was finished, he went into the house and found his wife dead.

Uncle Tom's wife had been a good piano player. She used to play for him every evening, and he was never allowed to forget that he had not gone for a doctor when she was so sick. Every night, after her death, the piano would play, very loudly, all by itself. Finally, he was driven insane and had to be put in an asylum.

13. The Tragedy at the Spring

SAM WALTON was a brutal, insanely jealous man. His wife Emily was a timid, frail woman, a bride of three summers,

whose time was spent with one thought in mind—the making
of a happy home for her moody, ungrateful husband. Their
log cabin home was up an isolated hollow, a mile from
the nearest road, where the neighboring farmers hauled
their grain and produce to the village about four miles
away.

Sam knew Emily was pure and faithful, but it served
his purpose to accuse her of being too friendly with the
son of their nearest neighbor, who occasionally came over to
help with the plowing and spring seeding. It helped to
provide a smokescreen for an affair with a young German
girl, the adopted daughter of Henry Schneider, who lived
about a quarter of a mile up the hollow. Sam often went
to town late in the afternoon and came home after dark, so
that he might meet the flaxen-haired Hilda.

One evening, Emily delayed milking later than usual,
and when she went to the barnyard, she found that one of
her three cows had not come in with the others. She
milked the two cows and then started out through the
pasture toward the west gate next to the woods. She did
not call, for she had found that late in the evening the
cows would often stop feeding in order to still their bells
and keep from being found.

And so it was that Emily, walking on the thick grass,
was close upon the guilty lovers before they were aware
of her approach. They could do nothing but crouch in
the shadows, waiting. Just then a cowbell tinkled and
Emily turned out of the path and down the hill where
Brindle stood quietly chewing her cud. She drove the cow
to the milking lot, unaware of the fright she had given the
guilty couple.

Finally Hilda broke the silence. "Do you think she saw
us?"

"I don't know. We can never be sure, damn it," Sam
said. "There is only one thing to do to be sure. You run
home and keep mum, and I'll do the rest."

Taking a roundabout way, Sam reached the spring

beyond the house. He knew Emily always went for water to wash the dishes and her milk pails.

"This will be her last trip for water," he said. "She brought it all on herself by her cursed snooping around."

Hidden by branches and the dark, he waited. A flood of light from the opened door told him his wife was starting to the spring. He crouched in the spruce thicket that surrounded the spring. A sudden breeze moved the branches slightly and a sighing like that of a departing spirit caused his flesh to creep and his blood to chill.

Now he could hear Emily's footsteps, and her slight form emerged from the shadows. As she knelt to dip the water, his hand grabbed her hair and a sharp blade slashed across her throat. A sharp, wailing cry pierced the silence of the night, but only once, for the murderer pressed her head into the spring, stifling all but a gurgling sound which soon stopped. Breathlessly, Sam Walton gazed upon the still body of his dead wife. He knew his job was not finished. He must hide the body, and hide it well.

Below the spring was a large pond fed by the spring. A few blows with a mattock and the pond was drained, and ten minutes of work with a spade excavated a shallow grave. It took but a moment to place the slight body in the watery tomb and cover it with the cold mud. In a short time the break in the wall was mended.

"By morning," thought Sam, "the pond will be full again. I will be safe."

Two days later he reported the disappearance of his wife; he said she had threatened to leave him, and one night he came home and she was gone.

"Just a little domestic trouble," folks thought. "Everything will turn out all right."

But things did not go well with Sam. He went about his work as usual, but he could not sleep. Often he heard queer sounds coming from the kitchen early in the morning —sounds like those Emily had made preparing breakfast.

At the evening milking, the cows seemed restless and

would sometimes stampede from the milking lot. For many days Walton would not go near the spring, although he had removed all traces of blood and had cleaned the spring thoroughly and limed it to purify the water. However, as weeks passed, he felt more at ease and started going to the spring again. It was much better water than he had been getting from the old wet-weather spring under the willow tree in the garden.

One night he went for water later than usual. The night was cloudy, and there was no moon. Sam felt ill at ease. The wind played upon the spruce branches, reminding him of the last exhalation of breath as the soul flies from the body. Then there was a soul-rending scream. Sam gave a hoarse cry and fled. He never knew when he passed the house. He only knew he fled in mortal fear.

The next summer, for the first time, the spring went dry. The pond, of course, dried up too. Early in the fall a neighbor boy was passing through the farm. His dog began digging in the soft mud in the bottom of the pond. The boy noticed a piece of cloth and tugged on it. When it would not come loose, he took a sharp stick and in a short time found that the cloth was on a human body. He reported the find, and the body was dug up. The mysterious disappearance of Emily Walton was solved.

Sam Walton was later found, and he made a full confession of the murder. At his trial he was judged insane and was committed to an institution, where he spent the remainder of his life.

Afterward no one would live on the farm. Weird noises were heard in the vicinity of the spring. The moaning of the wind in the spruce boughs sounded like a plaintive lament. Between eight and nine, any summer evening, a strange gurgling could be heard. Then a shrieking cry would pierce the silence, and the birds, frightened, would scud off into the night. Neighbors said that every year, on the anniversary of the killing, the crystal spring water changed to the color of blood.

22

14. *The Blue Boy Hotel*

THIS STORY is said to have happened between the years 1870 and 1895, on Main Street in Shinnston.

The setting was a two-story hotel, called the Blue Boy Hotel, which had a saloon in the front and a poolroom in the basement. Behind the hotel was a huge barn where all the livestock was kept. Bill and Melvin Everette were the owners.

These men would take in many guests during the year, most of whom were rich or well-to-do. If they had very large sums of money, Melvin knew it, because it was a house rule for the people to tell him how much money they had. He would get them into poker games, playing with a large sum of his own money so that the guests would keep playing. He often arranged to have a man or group of men come in and hold up the game. He would never be suspected because he played with a large amount of his own money.

Bill would court the women that came to the hotel. If they were rich, he would usually marry them. Then after a couple of weeks, he would kill his new wife and bury her under the barn, saying that she had left him.

The two brothers also rustled cattle and hid them at a farm at Adamsville until the brands were changed. Bill would then sell them to cattle buyers for a very reasonable price. But after each sale he would try to kill the buyer, take the cattle, and sell them again.

After a life of swindling, cheating, rustling, and murder, Bill died around 1890. Every night, after Bill's death, Melvin would dream about all the money Bill had. In the dream, Bill was hiding his money, but Melvin never found out where. One night as Melvin was getting ready to go to bed, his brother's ghost appeared. Bill told him to go to the old abandoned Lucky Lady mine, and then he disappeared. Melvin ran to the mine and got the money packs. Before he could reach the entrance again, he was covered by a slate fall.

The money was found beside Melvin's body. Inside the packs was a note, signed by Bill, saying that if anything should happen to Melvin the money was to go to Melvin's wife.

Not wanting the hotel and unable to sell it, Mrs. Everette had it torn down. When the barn was torn down, the bodies and skeletons of the murdered people were found.

When he heard what had been discovered under the barn, Aleza Driscal of Bluefield, whose daughter had disappeared while she was in Shinnston, came to town. Believing that his daughter had been killed by the brothers, he went to see Mrs. Everette and courted her. As a form of revenge, he took her out one night, shot her, and threw her body into the West Fork River.

Every night thereafter Mrs. Everette would appear to Mr. Driscal. He would see her walking in the garden, moving about in the house, and going down the street.

One rainy night he decided to walk down near the river. Reaching the river, he began to cry from shame. The ghost of Mrs. Everette was always with him, walking alongside him. He jumped into the West Fork and drowned himself. The bodies of Mrs. Everette and Mr. Driscal were found the next morning by the riverbank where Mr. Driscal had jumped in.

The ground was wet, and Mr. Driscal's footprints were clearly seen—down to the riverbank. And alongside his footprints were a set of woman's footprints, a set like those that could have been made only by the shoes Mrs. Everette was wearing.

3   Ghostly Children

IT IS HARD TO believe that so many children have been murdered or abused to the point of death without anyone to help them. Yet the greater part of the stories of ghost children I have collected depict such circumstances.

Naturally, these little ghosts come back in anger—to protest—although most of my adult ghosts are happy, even after violent deaths. Perhaps comparatively few children have died, except through neglect or murder, and nobody can blame a murdered child for being unhappy. Even so, this murder of children—and judging by my collection as a whole, the victims seem to be mostly babies—is a little hard to understand.

The young girl in "Help," though an exception to the element of cruelty, represents another common theme—the return of a ghost to help in an emergency. In *Bluenose Ghosts* (pp. 185-86), Helen Creighton tells a somewhat similar story, in which a long-dead mother summons a

priest to give absolution to her profligate son who dies later
that same night.

15. *The Little Rag Doll*

DUSK WAS beginning to fall over a little country community.
A tired schoolteacher was grading papers and looking
over some of the work for the following day.

It had been a beautiful day and, although her school
board and also her landlady had asked her not to stay after
school hours, she could not resist this urge to stay and work
a little longer. After all, they would not explain their
strange request, so she thought nothing was really meant
by it.

Suddenly she felt something cold, like a chill, pass over
her from head to foot. She felt an unknown fear, and
something told her to look at the back of the dreary school-
room.

Her startled eyes saw a little ragged girl sitting in the
third row—last seat back. She had her hand raised and was
looking pitifully at the teacher.

"Please show me my lesson in my primer, and, Teacher,"
she said in a broken voice, "I can't find my little rag doll."

The teacher went back to the child and was astonished
to see an old-fashioned primer, which had been used many
years before. She was so amazed that she just stood there
staring at the little girl, and the child vanished from the
room.

The schoolteacher told her landlady about it later that
evening. The landlady told her that this ghost had haunted
the school for many years, and the school board could not
find a teacher who would remain any length of time after
seeing the little girl. They were in desperate need of a
teacher, so they had asked her not to stay after school
hours, hoping that she would never see the ghost.

The teacher made a rag doll that night and decided about what assignment she would make if the little girl appeared again.

The next evening she intentionally remained after school hours. The little girl did appear and made the same request again. The teacher assigned the lesson and gave the child the little rag doll. The little girl then vanished as before.

The teacher and the landlady went for a walk that evening and finally came to a swamp. Many years ago, the landlady said, a little girl had been murdered there. She was on her way home from school and dusk was falling as she passed through the swamp. Her friends and relatives had never been able to find the little rag doll or the murderer.

When they arrived at the child's grave, they were both amazed to find, lying on the grave, the little rag doll the schoolteacher had made the night before for the little ghost girl.

The little girl never visited the school after that, and, evidently, her spirit is now at rest.

16. Help

MANY YEARS AGO Doctor Anderson was awakened by a persistent knocking at his front door. Accustomed to getting calls at all hours, he dressed quickly and hurried downstairs.

The red glow from the hearth cast flickering shadows through the room. Glancing at the large wall clock, he noticed it was just past midnight. Outside the moon shone brightly on the white snow.

He opened the door and was surprised to see a young girl twelve or thirteen years old standing before him. He had never seen her before. She was dressed in a blue coat, carried a white muff, and her cheeks were ruddy from the cold.

"Please come to my mother," begged the girl. "She's sick, and I'm afraid she'll die."

"Who is your mother?" asked the doctor.

"Mrs. Ballard," replied the girl. "Please hurry."

Then the girl explained that they had only recently moved to the old Hostler place about three miles away. She said she thought her mother had pneumonia, and since her father was dead, there was no one else to come for help.

When the doctor said that he would come at once and do all he could, the girl darted away, running up the road in the direction of the old Hostler place.

Doctor Anderson bundled up in his sheepskin coat, pulled down the earflaps of his cap, picked up his bag, and went to the barn for his horse. He lost no time in throwing on the bridle and saddle, picking up a blanket because it was "blue cold," and heading for the Hostler place, for in those days pneumonia was a dreaded illness.

As he hurried his horse up the cold snow-covered road, he kept thinking of the bravery of the young girl who had faced the severe cold to seek his help. She had run off before he could ask her in to warm herself, yet she hadn't appeared to be cold.

His thoughts soon turned to his own discomfort, because his feet and hands began to feel numb before he saw the glow of a lamp in the old Hostler house.

Quickly tying his horse to the gatepost, he threw the blanket over it and hurried up the snow-covered walk to the porch. There was no answer to his knock, so he opened the door and walked in. The sight was a common one to him. There in a bed lay the sick woman. The fire was almost out, but the oil lamp still burned. He felt the woman's pulse and found that she had a very high fever.

He placed more wood on the fire because the room was cold, then set to work with confidence that comes from having handled many emergencies. He knew if he could break the fever, he could possibly save the woman's life.

After giving her medicine, he heated water and applied poultices to her chest. She soon rallied enough to ask, "How did you know to come?"

The doctor replied that her daughter had come for him and that she was a brave girl to go out on such a bitter night.

"But I have no daughter," whispered the woman. "My daughter has been dead for three years."

"What!" exclaimed the doctor. "Why a young girl twelve or thirteen years old called me out of bed and begged me to hurry here."

"It couldn't have been my daughter. She died from pneumonia three years ago."

"Who could it have been then?" asked the doctor. "And how did she know you were ill? She was dressed in a blue coat and white muff."

"My daughter had a blue coat and white muff," whispered the woman. "They're hanging in the closet over there."

Doctor Anderson strode over to the closet, opened the door, and took out a blue coat and white muff. His hands trembled when he felt the coat and muff and found them still warm and damp from perspiration.

17. The Baby in the Fireplace

Mrs. Anne Bennett once lived in a house that had a haunted fireplace. She said every night about seven o'clock they could hear a low, baby's voice saying, "Help! Help!" This would continue for about five minutes, and then they could see a baby's face that looked as if it were in great pain. That too would go away, and nothing would be seen or heard until the next night.

They decided to tear down the fireplace and take the chimney down to see if that would stop the mysterious cries. When they got it all down, they found baby bones. They buried them, and never heard the noise or saw the face after that.

Later they found out that a man had beaten his baby to death for crying and had put the body in the fireplace to burn.

18. Rapping on the Door

YEARS AGO, the mother of a small boy locked him in a closet as a punishment. The boy had always been afraid of the dark and yelled and screamed at the top of his voice. Finally he tried to climb over the door and push himself through an opening where a board had once been.

Just as he was about to get through, he slipped and fell and broke his neck; as he died, he knocked on the wall as a last attempt to get help. When the mother finally came to let out her son, she found him dead.

A few weeks later, late at night, she heard a rapping at the door. Every night after that, she heard this noise. Her husband, who was afraid his wife would lose her mind, decided that they should move.

After they left, some other people moved in and they, too, every once in a while would hear a faint rapping at the closet door. Finally the rapping stopped, just as if the boy had finally given up trying to get out.

19. The Boy and the Trumpet

A YOUNG BOY's parents were very strict with him and wouldn't allow him to do much of anything. He had always wanted to play a trumpet, but his father and mother said they didn't have the money to get him one, although they seemed to be able to afford other things.

One day the boy's aunt came to visit them and found out how badly he wanted a horn and how unlikely it was that he would ever have one. Sometime later, after his aunt had gone back home, the boy received a large package in the mail. Like any child, he was very excited about getting a package. But, when he opened it and found a brand-new trumpet, with a note from his aunt saying she hoped he would like it and learn to play, he was more excited than ever and thought he could now learn to play.

His parents, though, were disgusted and refused to let him take lessons. The boy begged and pleaded, but it did no good. After that, he wasn't much interested in anything and grew thin and pale. When the mother would ask him what was wrong, he would just say, "Nothing; only someday, I hope I can play."

One night, when his mother went in to tell him goodnight, he was dead. She screamed and as she turned to run and tell his father, a little skeleton walked up beside her, playing the sweetest music she'd ever heard. The father heard the music and his wife screaming and came to see what was wrong. He, too, saw the skeleton playing the horn. Then he saw his son was dead and went over to the bedside. When he turned back around, the skeleton had disappeared.

The mother told the father that they were the cause of the boy's death—that they had denied him everything he'd really wanted and he was just too sick at heart to live. When they went out in the hall, the skeleton was down at the far end, playing again, but he stopped for a second and spoke. He said he'd be around to take the place of their son and make sure they didn't forget him. Then he turned and went back into the boy's room.

No one else ever saw the skeleton, and most of the

neighbors believed the parents were so conscience-stricken that they'd just imagined they had.

20. *The Running Child*

THE FIRST TIME my great-aunt and great-uncle bought a home of their own, they were very pleased, although they had been warned of strange things that happened in the house. Paying no attention to these warnings, they fixed up the old place. While she was cleaning the floors, my great-aunt found a reddish stain in front of the coat closet. Though she scrubbed and scrubbed it, she could not get it out and finally she covered it neatly with a rug and soon forgot all about it.

The first night the family slept in their new home, they were suddenly all awakened by the sound of a running child's footsteps. The child seemed to run through the hall and down the stairs to the coat closet and then to bang its hands on the closet door. They all jumped out of bed and went to see what was happening, but they could find nothing. For about a month they would hear these strange sounds every night.

At that time my great-uncle took a job in the mines at Pierce, and so the family moved away from the house and those disturbing noises.

The story they heard later was that an insane man had killed his small child in front of the coat closet after having chased it all through the house.

4   Murdered Kinsmen

NONE OF THE victims of these unnatural murders come back with good intentions, but rather with ill will in their hearts for their relative murderers. Who can blame them? Murdering one's own flesh and blood is traditionally one of the most repugnant crimes, and a father who kills his own son for drinking up all the wine deserves just what he got. Brothers seem to be particularly murderous of each other in West Virginia, but for that matter "fraticide punished" has been a popular literary theme, at least since the twelfth century.

21.   The Glass Jug

MR. PECK had beaten his son to death, because he drank up all his wine. The day of the son's funeral he told the people he'd fallen and killed himself, and nobody knew but what this was true.

That night, after the funeral, Mr. Peck decided to go down town and buy himself a drink or two. On his way home he could hear something beside him, but couldn't see anything. He went on a little farther and saw a jug, tipped up, walking beside him. It seemed as if someone were drinking out of it.

Then a voice said, "Thirsty, Pop?" and repeated this over and over.

Frightened, Mr. Peck grabbed the jug and broke it against his chest. A piece of the glass cut his throat badly, and as he was getting very weak, the voice said, "I'm still here, Pop."

Then Mr. Peck fell over and bled to death.

22. *Chop Chop*

IN SOME families the good and evil are not properly balanced. Instead of being two ordinary boys with a lot of good in them and a few faults, the Harrison brothers were exact opposites. One was quite good and one was quite bad.

The boys' father passed away and left the farm, which had been in the family for generations, to the two unmarried sons. When the good brother wanted to sell his half, the bad one grew angry and killed him with a hatchet. After the murder he simply put his brother's body under the floor. To cap his crime, the bad brother wooed and wedded the deceased one's girl.

On the first night after the marriage, his troubles started. The trouble was—a steady chop, chop, chop. Every time he approached his wife, the noise would start. The frightened girl, after a week in the house, begged her

husband to leave with her. He refused and tried to kill her. Escaping, she rushed to the neighbors for help.

Returning to the house, they found the bad brother had hanged himself, after opening the floor to look at the body. Beside the dead good brother was a hatchet.

23. Rose Run

FAR BACK on Bunner's Ridge close to Morgantown, there is a "run," as all of the little valleys in this area are called. It was and still is referred to as Rose Run. The name came from the wild roses that once covered the valley and choked out everything.

In this small valley once dwelt some of the better-off farmers of the ridge. One of the richer, prouder farmers had a beautiful daughter whose name was Rose. In spite of her father's objections, she loved a city boy. One night while she was with her lover at a dance, her father shot at the young man. But the bullet hit and killed Rose.

The father swore the young man had killed her. The other farmers naturally believed him, and the young man was hanged shortly afterward. Still filled with bitterness, the father took the girl's body and buried it in a remote spot on his farm.

Soon, however, from her grave sprang a multitude of wild roses that seemed to spread like wildfire, choking the very sunlight from the soil. In a short time the whole farm was covered, and then the valley too. The roses are gone now, but the story remains.

24. The Brother and His Horse

IN SOUTHERN West Virginia, there is a house standing on the most prominent point in the country. It is a large, two-story, frame house, with stone chimneys and a fireplace in every room. Just outside the kitchen door is an unusually large well, dug by pick and shovel and lined with rock. A long lane, lined with a number of large pine trees, leads to the house. When there is a slight wind blowing, the whistling of the trees can be heard quite a distance away.

Two brothers once lived in the house. Their parents had left them well-off, but the brothers constantly quarreled and argued over which of them would finally get the farm. On the farm the brothers had a team of fine workhorses. One of these horses, a huge white animal, was the younger brother's favorite. He showed him special attention, currying him and giving him special tidbits to eat, and the horse seemed equally fond of his master.

One day the brothers were arguing, and the older brother knocked the younger one unconscious. He then placed him on his favorite horse and forced the horse to jump into the well. The older brother was immediately suspected of killing his younger brother, but not enough proof could be gathered for his arrest and conviction. He was free to claim ownership of all the money and the farm too.

The brother lived by himself and managed the farm. One day as a group of young men were walking on the road past the house, they noticed that there was no smoke coming from the chimneys. This was strange because it was late in the fall and quite cold. They decided to investigate and found the house completely empty. It seemed as if someone had just left the house, but there was no sign of the brother.

It was getting dark when the men decided to go to town and report the missing man. On their way out the long lane leading to the house, they heard a sound like the galloping of a horse. They looked up and saw a white glow approaching them. As the glow came closer, they could recognize the outline of a horse ridden by a young man. Behind the rider was a limp object wrapped in a burlap sack. The horseman came within fifty yards of the frightened group and dropped his bundle. Then both horse and rider disappeared into the air.

When the men gathered enough courage to approach the fallen bundle, they found the older brother wrapped in the burlap. There was no trace that a horse had ever been there. Although there were flakes of snow on the ground, no horse's track could be found anywhere.

Some people still say that the younger brother and his horse can be heard galloping across the hill at dusk by anyone courageous enough to walk the long lane leading to the now deserted house.

25. *The Shadow on the Wall*

EARL RIGGS lived in an old house with his housekeeper, Martha, after his brother Ned died. Earl wouldn't leave the house after the funeral, and during the night, Martha could hear him come into the hall. It sounded to her as if he were washing the wall or something. She decided to open the door to see what he was doing, and there he was scrubbing down the hall wall. She was worried about this and wrote to his sister Mary about him. Mary received the letter and came as soon as she could.

That night Mary told Martha that they'd watch to see what he would do. About midnight they heard him come out and start washing again. Mary ran to him and asked why he was doing that, but he told them to leave him alone and not to look at what he was doing. Mary looked anyway, and there on the wall was the shadow of their brother Ned.

When Earl saw that they had seen this, he told them all about it. He said he had given Ned poison, and, every night after that, he would see this shadow and had to wash it away.

5   Omens of Death

THERE IS AN old superstition that white animals are omens
of death, and three of the stories in this section are
representative of this belief. The most frequently used
animal is a white horse. Perhaps the prominence of the
horse in this connection goes back to the common depiction
of death on a white horse, a notable example appearing in
Revelation in the Bible. Vance Randolph in *Ozark Superstitions* also has a story illustrating the white horse theme.

From the stories it is not always easy to tell whether
these are spectral creatures or whether they are actual
animals. The white dog and the white stallion are possibly
real creatures, though one cannot be certain. Shiny Eyes
and the white horse, on the other hand, are obviously
spectral animals.

26. The Gate

ABOUT HALFWAY back on Bunner's Ridge the road separates a haunted house and a cemetery. People passing the house, even in this day and age, feel strange. In former times some even thought they felt evil spirits acting on them when they got close to the place. A very old woman lived in the house until her death a few years ago. She was the reason for it all.

Early in her life her husband Bert had built the house as a wedding gift, but in the second year of their marriage he was struck by the fever. The neighbors were so sure of his death, they dug his grave in the cemetery across the road. Bert, however, did not die right away.

During his illness a strange thing happened. A visitor leaving the house one night heard a strange rattling sound in the cemetery. Frightened by this report, the woman went to an Indian doctor to discover what it was all about. The doctor decided it was the Angel of Death and it would not be satisfied until the grave was filled.

She tried to appease the angel by filling up the grave, but the rattling continued. The doctor then sprinkled the cemetery fence with a dust that would keep the angel in the cemetery at night. He cautioned everyone to keep the gates to the cemetery field closed—especially at night.

Bert still remained in serious condition, so the woman had to sit up every night with him and listen to the terrible rattling as the angel paced along the fence of the cemetery. Soon her nerves could stand it no longer, and she knew she must move Bert. The next day she arranged for an ambulance to move him to the hospital in Morgantown.

That night she went to bed as soon as it got dark, relieved that she could rest in peace. Soon the strange noise came closer to the fence of the cemetery. Much to her horror the noise seemed to come right through the fence and hurry off down the road toward Morgantown.

41

The next day the drivers of the hearse from the hospital found her sobbing at the open gate, where she had been all night. "He's dead! He's dead!"

The hearse wasn't as long as the ambulance, so the driver didn't have to open the cemetery gate to turn around as the ambulance driver did when he took Bert away.

27. Shiny Eyes

MY FATHER, born in Italy and the oldest of four children, decided to do something to help the family, and in 1913 he came to the United States. Relatives from the Pennsylvania coalfields were waiting in New York City, to take him back with them. They found him a job, and he immediately went to work in an anthracite mine, located in Ligonier, Pennsylvania, and owned and operated by a Colonel Thomas.

During the first year that he worked at the drift mine, a strange animal started appearing. It would walk to the mouth of the slope, look inside, then turn around and go back to its lair in the mountain. About fifteen minutes after the animal had appeared, two or three men would get killed by a slate fall.

The animal was about eight feet long, five feet high, and about the same color as a mouse. It had two large eyes that shone like the headlights of a powerful automobile. Because of its two large eyes, the animal came to be known as Shiny Eyes. As many as ten men at one time had shot at it as it slowly and warily walked from the mountain to the mine and then from the mine back to the mountain. They could not seem to hurt or kill Shiny Eyes because it would just turn around, look at the men who were shooting at it, and then proceed to its mountain lair.

This began to trouble the miners as well as the mine owner. Something had to be done to rid the community of the bad luck which Shiny Eyes was causing. The only solution was to get rid of Shiny Eyes. Colonel Thomas thought that he could make the necessary arrangements to do this.

He made a deal with two brothers, Bill and Jack Robinson, who were supposed to be the meanest men in the mining town. He offered each of them three hundred dollars in cash if they would kill Shiny Eyes. He would also give each one of them a high-powered rifle, a jug of whisky, and pay them a day's wages. The two brothers accepted the offer, got their supplies together, and proceeded to a small shack that was located along the trail that Shiny Eyes always used. There they waited for it to appear, but before long, they had consumed their whisky and were drunk. Jack decided to go into town to purchase another gallon of whisky and left Bill at the shack to watch for Shiny Eyes.

While Jack was gone, Bill fell asleep. He was suddenly awakened by a loud noise at the door. He looked up and fainted at the sight of Shiny Eyes. There it was, standing in the doorway with its two shining eyes brightly glaring. It was not concerned with Bill and proceeded to the mine. When Jack returned to the shack, he found Bill lying on the floor. He revived Bill, and the two then prepared to shoot Shiny Eyes as it returned to the mountain.

Meanwhile, Shiny Eyes had gone to the mine and walked down the slope about fifty yards, turned around, and walked out. When it got outside, it looked down the slope once more. It then turned around and started walking back to its mountain lair. As it started up the mountain trail, Bill and Jack started shooting at it, but the bullets from the high-powered rifles did not seem to bother it. About an hour after Shiny Eyes appeared, the mine exploded and twenty-two men were killed. This was the worst explosion that had ever occurred at the mine, but afterward Shiny Eyes was neither seen nor heard of again.

28. The White Horse

THERE WAS a white horse which roamed the hills around
Mason at night, and anyone who saw it was sure to die.
No one would ever go far into the hills after sundown,
because everyone was afraid of the horse.

One Fourth of July, George Miller rode into town and
stopped in front of the town's gambling house. He went in
and sat down at the card table and played cards until late
at night. While he was playing cards, he drank whisky
and kept on until he was drunk.

At about 2:30 in the morning the card game broke up,
so George started for home. Since it was so late, he took a
shortcut through the woods. He got about halfway home,
and then in the distance he saw a big, bright light.

The light got brighter and brighter, and came closer
and closer, and all of a sudden, he saw the white horse.
He tried to ride away, but it was too late. The spell of the
white horse had already done its work, and George rolled
from his horse, dead.

Since that time, the people of Mason have closed all
parts of the woods so that no one can go in there.

29. The White Stallion

AROUND 1900 in a house located in a lonely hollow east of
Route 57 in Barbour County, an old man named Gall was
sick in bed and was about to pass away. His family was
gathered at the farm to be with him in his last hours.

Just after midnight those attending the elderly man
noticed that a white stallion had come over the hill and was
heading toward the house. When the brilliant, pale-colored
horse was close to the house, he circled it cautiously. He

44

then went off in the same direction from which he had come, trotttng up the side of the hill.

The white stallion disappeared over the top of the hill. As he vanished over the crest, the old man died. This was the first and last time that a white stallion was seen in that particular part of the country.

30. White Death

ESTHER, MY father's younger sister, was in bed recovering from the chickenpox. She had been in bed for three days, but was rapidly improving.

While she was sick, strange cries could be heard during the night from far off in the distance, but in the morning they would stop. Her parents thought the noise was the sound of a stray wolf and paid no further attention to it. Then for three days in a row, a large white dog appeared outside of Esther's window.

On the fourth day Esther's mother was in the room feeding her a bowl of soup. The big white dog suddenly jumped through the open window, licked Esther's hand, and then disappeared. Five minutes later Esther was dead! It was strange, because only that morning the doctor had said she could get out of bed in another day or so.

31. A Ride with the Devil

ONE DARK evening, about one hundred years ago, my great-grandfather had a strange experience. He was riding his horse back from a small country store somewhere in Randolph County in the vicinity of Mill Creek. He heard something that sounded like a log chain falling from a tree, and then he felt the presence of something on the horse behind him.

He was frightened half out of his wits, but he turned his head around to see what the thing was. First he saw long claws that were digging into the flesh on his shoulder. He thought that a bear had jumped behind him on his horse, but, turning his head farther around, he found himself staring straight into two fire-red eyes. The creature had hardly any nose, but there were two protruding objects on his head that looked like horns. He was face to face with Satan himself! He tried many times to shake him off his back. He pushed. He tried racing his horse to get rid of him. But all this did no good. Satan clung to his back with those razorlike claws through it all.

As he came within sight of his home, a strange thing happened. To his utter surprise, the thing disappeared.

Upon arriving home, he slowly walked into the house. His wife noticed his torn shirt and bleeding shoulder and was terrified.

He told her the whole story, but asked her never to say anything about it to anyone. Then he said something else. He said, "I have just seen the devil, and it won't be long now before he gets me."

Exactly three weeks from that chance meeting with the devil, Grandfather fell while repairing his tobacco shed and was killed almost instantly. His last word before he died was "Water!"

6   Deadly Visions

Death warnings, usually in the form of dreams or sudden visions of a person who is ill or absent, are particularly interesting, since there can be little doubt of the sincerity of the teller of such experiences. Such experiences have been reported down through the ages and retold by poets including Chaucer and Shakespeare.

Many people have reported death knocks and dream warnings, including Dr. Helen C. Creighton in her introduction to *Bluenose Ghosts*. I, too, have had a number of dream warnings, including dreams of telegrams whose unusual wording was repeated exactly some time later in real telegrams. Two of these dream warnings took place before the deaths of my uncle and mother. I realize that there is a possible psychological explanation of my dreams, since I was under considerable stress at the time. Nevertheless, the repetition of out-of-the-ordinary details is a little hard to explain, and besides it's more interesting to think of them as possible supernatural experiences.

In the section on ghost stories in Emelyn E. Gardner's *Folklore from the Schoharie Hills, New York* (pp. 85-97), there are a number of death warnings, such as death knocks, balls of fire, a bright light, a woman in white, a black figure, a vision of a sick woman, a clock that started to run and strike—although it had not run for years—and the appearance of a coffin the right size for a neighbor man who died that same day. Harry M. Hyatt, in *Folk-Lore from Adams County, Illinois,* devotes a number of pages to death warnings.

32. *A Dream*

In 1900, WHEN my father was about eighteen, he attended Glenville State Teachers' College, then known as Glenville Normal School. Daddy roomed in the old Whiting House in Glenville with a friend named Will.

One weekend Daddy left Glenville for a visit to his home, up Bear Run. He arrived there at about 8 p.m. and, as was the custom, retired at about 9 p.m.

At midnight Daddy awoke from a horrible dream, in which he had seen his roommate open the door to their room in the hotel in Glenville and walk to the top of the stairs. At that instant a shot rang out from below, and Will tumbled head over heels to the bottom of the steps. He was dead when he landed at the bottom.

Next morning at breakfast Daddy told about his dream. He was very depressed. The family paid little attention to the dream, but Daddy felt that something must be wrong, for the dream had seemed so real. My grandfather went to town that day. Imagine his surprise when he heard, immediately upon his arrival, the same story Daddy had told at the breakfast table. This time, however, it was not a dream. Will had been killed exactly as Daddy dreamed it, and at exactly the same time of night.

33. Grandfather's Clock

GRANDFATHER ROBEY had retired early on that fateful evening of April 14, 1865, because he was tired. He was more than tired. Things hadn't gone too well. His work had seemed more difficult than usual, and the children were more fretful.

Grandfather was exceptionally tired that evening. He could think of nothing that was cheerful. The children had mislaid his tools, and he had reprimanded them and ordered them to bed early. But rest was not to be had. There seemed to be a cloud of premonition over all. Grandmother, glad of a few minutes' peace, did some mending, sitting by the candlelight in the rocking chair he had made for her.

Suddenly, Grandfather sprang out of bed, horror-stricken, looking about him as though he didn't recognize any familiar surroundings. Grandmother, never one to get excited without just cause, waited patiently for him to speak, continuing meanwhile to stitch calmly on the sock heel she was mending.

"My God, Rose Ann, Abraham Lincoln was just shot!" he exclaimed.

"Now, Thomas," said Grandmother soothingly, "you've been having a bad dream."

"No, Rose Ann, I tell you, I was there! I saw it happen! He was mortally wounded!"

Grandmother was now impressed. There could be no doubt that he had indeed been through a shattering experience.

Grandfather, now thoroughly awake and aroused, began to pace the floor. On a sudden impulse, he stopped in front of the mantel clock and marked the position of the hands. Also, he noted on it the month and the day in small figures.

The news from the East reached Clarksburg by stagecoach some two weeks later. It was learned that on the exact day and hour marked on the face of the clock by Grandfather Robey, John Wilkes Booth had indeed fired one shot into the back of the Great Emancipator, mortally wounding him.

This clock remained in the Robey family for many decades.

34. Death Warning

MY GREAT AUNT, whose daughter had been seriously ill for many weeks, retired one evening to get a little rest. She was lying on her bed in the dark, but had not dropped off to sleep. Suddenly, she was aware that someone was coming up the stairs from the first floor to the second. Her room was very dark, but she saw a figure in white come into her room and go into her daughter's room. She heard the apparition open a dresser drawer and later close it.

The figure retreated in the same manner in which it had come. However, it appeared to be carrying a piece of her daughter's clothing across its outstretched arms. She heard the downstairs door open and close as it left the house. She was terror-stricken, but was afraid to move out of her bed. Finally, she concluded that possibly she had dreamed the incident because of her exhaustion and worry.

The following night the same thing happened again. This time she was sure she had not dreamed, but had actually seen the apparition. Still, she declined to mention the incident, not wishing to worry the family further.

On the third night, she again heard the footsteps, saw the figure go through her room into her daughter's room and return, retreating down the steps in the same manner as on the other two nights. She heard the door open and then close. She immediately decided she would get out of bed and see if she could see the figure leave the house. The moon was bright, and she very plainly saw the figure cross the street and go up the steps of the church which was just across the street. She saw the apparition pass by the church and go into the churchyard.

On the following night, her daughter died. The services were held in the church across the street, and she was buried in the churchyard.

35. The Voice in the Night

WHEN I WAS a boy, I thought there was nothing in the world so good to eat as honey. Since I never got enough of it, I never got tired of it. My cousin Bill had a lot of bees, and knowing how well I liked honey, he would send me word every year in May, when he robbed his bees, to come and get me some. No matter where I was or what I was doing, I would go, and he would bring out a big panful of honey, and I would sit down and eat all of it while he watched me and laughed.

He was good to me in many other ways, and I thought of him as an older brother, rather than just a cousin. In fact, I would have stayed with him all the time if my father would have let me. But as the years went by, I didn't see him so often, and almost before I knew it, he was an old man. When I heard, one day, that he was sick, I was ashamed of myself for not having been to visit him for so long, and I shut up my shop right away and started out for his house.

When I got there, I saw that he was very poorly. But he was glad to see me, and we talked all day about his bees, the amount of honey I used to eat, and the things we used to do together. When I had to leave, I took his hand and told him I wanted him to hurry and get well so he could come to see me. He smiled and said that he would stop and speak to me when he passed by.

I knew I would never see him again. I studied about him all the way home and thought I would never go to sleep that night. At last I did, only to wake up sometime in the night with the feeling that somebody had been calling my name. I sat up in bed and heard Bill's voice as plainly as if he had been standing there in the room. "Henry," he said, "I'm going."

That was all he said. I got up and looked at my watch and saw that it was 1:05 a.m. I worried through the rest of the night until, finally, it was morning and time to go down and open the shop. As I was going down the street, I met some of my cousin's neighbors. They asked me if I had heard that Bill was dead. I said yes, he had spoken to me when he passed by at five minutes after one. They looked at each other, very much surprised. That was exactly the time he had died, they said. They had been there, and they knew.

36. Vision in a Field

A MAN AND his son went over to hoe out a neighbor's cornfield. The neighbor was down sick with typhoid fever. He was burning up and begged for a drink of water from the spring up in the cornfield. In those times not one drop of water was given a typhoid patient for fear of killing him.

It was a hot day, and the two men stopped their hoeing as they passed by the spring, got a drink, and sat down in the shade to rest a few minutes. Suddenly the son said, "Look, there comes Ef in his shirt-tail."

Ef came on to the spring, lay down on his stomach and drank for a long time, then vanished. Both men stared.

53

Finally the father said, "Ef won't get well. That was a token of his death."

They hoed on until evening. When they had finished and come off the hill, they found that Ef had died about the middle of the afternoon, just when they had seen him drink.

37. *Captain Copenhaver's Ghost*

FRANK COPENHAVER of my community went off to fight in the Civil War and became a captain.

His home was a two-room log cabin with double chimneys in each room and a big fireplace. In one room the family lived and slept. In the other they cooked and ate, and kept their food supplies. To lock the door they pulled in the latch string.

One unusually cold night they had a big, bright fire. Mrs. Copenhaver put her children to bed, sat and worked while her fire burned down, then retired herself. Because she was alone, she always made sure her latch strings were pulled in herself. This night she checked them as usual before going to bed.

As she lay there watching the fire, she heard footsteps come up to the door. Then the latch was lifted and in walked her husband. He was dressed in his army uniform, but it was spattered with blood. He walked to the fire and poked it up. His wife sprang from her bed and cried, "Frank, you've come home!"

This awoke the children, but their father was not there. The door was open and the poker lay on the floor where it had dropped when he vanished. Mrs. Copenhaver declared it was a token of something being wrong with her husband.

After the close of the war a neighbor, Wid Price, returned. He told how the two armies were camped so

54

close one time that they could see each other's campfires, which they kept burning all night long because of the severe cold. He also told of scouting parties slipping in from the enemy camp during the night, and always someone was killed. During one of these raids, their captain, Frank Copenhaver, was killed.

38. Christmas Tree

MR. AND MRS. Dennis Hostuttler were trying to get a tree for Christmas. Mr. Hostuttler had tried to buy one, but none of the trees he looked at suited his wife.

On the way home, Mrs. Hostuttler looked over in the cemetery and saw one of the prettiest trees she'd ever seen. She told Dennis to stop the car and go and get it. It was dark and no one would see them, she said.

Her husband wouldn't cut the tree at first, but she insisted, so he went in finally and cut it down. As the tree fell, it seemed as if a voice said, "I'll make you sorry."

Mr. Hostuttler put the tree on the car and started up the hill. As he got to the worst turn, he met a buggy and a man standing beside it. He got around them, but then he looked back and there was nothing there. The Hostuttlers went on over the ridge, and when they were almost home, they saw the same man and the same buggy again, but before they got to them, they went up the roadside, out of sight.

The Hostuttlers got home without further delay and put the tree up. Mrs. Hostuttler trimmed it and called the family in to see it. She stepped back to admire it, and there, in the top of the tree, was a little man and a buggy. She showed it to Dennis and said it was the same man they'd seen twice, on their way home.

Mrs. Hostuttler talked to the man and asked why he insisted on following them.

The man told her that he'd been killed in a buggy wreck and that, as long as the pine tree was on his grave, he'd had a chance to get to heaven, because he used to raise pine trees and give them away. But since she'd made her husband steal the tree—cut it down and take it from the cemetery—she'd suffer for it the rest of her life.

He said, "I'll leave now, but you don't have long to live either. By the time the pine tree is dead, you'll be in your grave."

And a month, to the day, after that, Mrs. Hostuttler died.

7   Headless Ghosts

THE HEADLESS ghost is undoubtedly one of the most popular figures in ghost stories, judging by the number of times he appears. In almost every collection of tales there will be one or more headless ghosts. This particular kind of ghost also illustrates the problem of arrangement that faces the collector. Actually, there are thirteen headless ghosts in this book—nine more than the four included in this section—but most of them seemed to go more naturally in some other category.

Perhaps the best known literary example is the headless horseman of Washington Irving's "The Legend of Sleepy Hollow." West Virginia has a number of these riders, but they have been omitted here, as other tales were more dramatically told. "The Headless Hant," in *The Book of Negro Folklore* (pp. 164-65) by Langston Hughes and Arna Bontemps, is an excellent example of a headless ghost.

39. Return of the Headless Man

ONE DAY AS the men were trying to clear a certain area of timber in the backwoods of Barbour County, a worker got too close to a circular saw. He saw his danger too late, and before he could move, the blade tore into his neck. Blood flew everywhere, spraying the surrounding trees and ground with a red blanket. The man's head dropped to the ground like a coconut from a tree. His body whirled three times and then fell against a hollow log.

No one could move, because everyone was stunned by the accident. After the men finally recovered from the shock, they made arrangements to have the mangled body removed to a funeral home. It was several months before the memory of the accident faded from their minds.

One night in the quiet logging camp, as a night watchman made the rounds, checking the equipment and watching for thieves, he saw the figure of a man standing in the exact spot of the accident. Caught by surprise, he froze for a few minutes. As soon as he had recovered sufficiently, he started walking toward the figure. He was shocked to see the same person that had been killed a few months before. Just then the figure disappeared, and the watchman turned and ran to town to report the headless man's return.

Night after night the same thing would happen. One night the watchman shot at the figure to see if that would stop him, but it didn't. The man would just vanish into the night.

Then, about a month later, a forest fire burned down all the woods, including the logging camp. So the loggers moved on to another location.

Just for curiosity the loggers came back to see if the man was still there. He wasn't. The general opinion of the woodsmen was that the dead man had gotten his revenge and now he was happy.

40. The Headless Rider

MANY YEARS ago, at a place called Pleasant Hill, a sparsely settled section of Doddridge County, there was a church and graveyard. At that time the church was new, and only a very few people had been buried there. But just over the edge of the hill was a dense clump of bushes, and in the center of this was a mound that looked much like a grave, a lonely grave. It was said that a traveler had been murdered and buried there, by whom, no one knew.

But at a certain time each month, when the moon was full, the ghost haunted the road in the form of a headless man. My great-uncle, though, had never believed any of these stories, as he had ridden this road all hours of the night and had seen no sign of this headless ghost. But one night as my great-uncle was coming home very late, his mare seemed to be weighted down with such a heavy load, she could hardly take a step. My uncle put his hand behind him, and felt a man's leg; then a heavy hand was placed on his leg. Looking around, he saw the headless man sitting behind him.

The mare took fright but could only struggle along slowly until they came opposite the mysterious grave; then the man disappeared. The mare ran all the way home, and from that time on it was almost impossible to ride her past that spot after dusk.

41. The Headless Husband

MRS. KERNS lived in Grant Town, where her husband worked in the mines. One day, in a mine accident, her neighbor's husband was killed—his head completely blown off—so Mrs. Kerns invited the widow to stay with her for a few days.

On the night after the funeral, Mrs. Kerns and her guest were sitting by the fire when they heard a knock outside. When Mrs. Kerns opened the door, the woman's dead husband walked in, with his head in his arms. Without saying a word, he walked through the house and out the back door. On the porch he dropped something. After he had gone off into the night, Mrs. Kerns locked the doors and windows.

When Mr. Kerns came home from work the next morning, he found a wedding band on the back porch. The neighbor woman said it was her dead husband's ring, which had been buried with him.

42. *The Old Well*

WHEN MY Uncle Harry was in his middle teens, each night after supper, like any young man, he would go to visit his girl, who lived about a mile away. One evening he started home later than usual. The sky was unusually dark, but occasionally the moon would pass from behind a cloud.

Since it was rather late, Uncle Harry decided to take a shortcut that led him past the old Barclay house, which had been deserted for nearly fifteen years.

While passing in front of the ghostly-looking old building, he heard a moaning sound coming from near the water well which was about ten feet from the house. Filled with curiosity, he opened the gate, which nearly collapsed behind him. As he slowly approached the well, the sound grew louder, and the beating of his heart grew more intense with every step.

Suddenly he saw a large, unrecognizable shadow behind the well. He approached hesitantly. By now the shadow had taken form. It was a man without a head, standing with an axe on his shoulder. For a few seconds, every muscle and bone in my uncle's body froze; then, he ran home as if all hell were after him.

For almost a week after the incident, my uncle tried to give every possible explanation for what had happened. He had finally convinced himself that his imagination had been playing tricks on him, when an old farmer told him he had once found a man's head near the old Barclay house. But the old farmer said he couldn't imagine where the body could be.

8   Hidden Money

CONSIDERING ALL the ghosts that return, or at least make themselves visible, for the sole purpose of pointing out hidden wealth, it seems that ghosts should be less feared and more appreciated. These money-minded ghosts go to a lot of trouble to help some living human being to a fortune, and they get very little for their pains. Perhaps it is as if they had the money in trust and cannot rest until they have fulfilled the trust by passing it along to someone who can use it.

The return of a spirit to reveal hidden treasure is one of the more popular themes in American ghost tales. John Harden, Louis C. Jones, Vance Randolph, and George Korson all include examples of it in their collections.

43. Footsteps on the Walk

MY GREAT-GRANDMOTHER was a very religious person. She did not believe in ghosts—at least so she claimed—but she did believe in the existence of spirits, which to her was quite a different thing. This story is about one of Great-grandmother's spirits.

In the small Pennsylvania town of Coburn, where she lived by herself in a small house, my great-grandmother's nearest neighbors were the Gibsons, people who were considered odd by the rest of the town. For although they were the owners of a rich coal mine, they lived in comparative poverty. Everyone said it was because old Lanham Gibson, the father, was a miser.

My great-grandmother wasn't one to gossip, and she probably was not exaggerating when she said the family quarreled a lot over money. She got all her information firsthand. After old Lanham lost his eyesight in an accident at the mine, he'd come to visit quite often, just to get out of his house. His family resented his miserliness and constantly hounded him about money.

My great-grandmother could tell he was coming by the sound of his footsteps and the tapping of the cane on the walk. She didn't mind his intrusion on her privacy, as he was usually complacent enough, as though seeking refuge from the rest of the world. In the evenings they would sit together on the big porch and enjoy the dusk. Grandma usually had her knitting with her, and old Lanham had his dingy old pipe.

One day, while out walking, Lanham missed a step and fell over an embankment, killing himself. He had left a large fortune behind, but it could not be located. The family searched and searched, but nothing ever came of it.

About a year later my great-grandmother was sitting on the porch with her knitting, enjoying the cool evening breeze, when she heard the familiar footsteps and the tapping of a cane on the walk. She looked up expectantly, but saw no one. The sound grew closer, and then stopped in front of her. Suddenly she heard a weird laugh; then all was quiet again.

This happened night after night, and finally, in despair, she went to the minister with her story. He told her that if it happened again, she was to repeat a certain verse from the Bible that was supposed to appease wandering spirits.

The very next night, when she heard the footsteps and the tapping of the cane, she read aloud the verse her minister had given her. Now, instead of the laughter, she heard a voice say, "The money's in the well."

The following day she went to the Gibson family and told them the story. An exploration of the well led to the discovery of one hundred and twelve thousand dollars in currency and gold. This the family proceeded to spend lavishly on themselves, and although they would never have found the money without my great-grandmother's help, they never offered her anything.

After their first fling, the Gibsons put the remaining money in a safety deposit box in the bank. A few weeks later, on returning to the box for more money, they discovered it was empty. This brought about a thorough check of the other deposit boxes and of the bank's funds. It was finally determined that nothing else was missing and that apparently the box had not been opened. The family never recovered from the blow, and lived out their lives in poverty.

44. The Haunted House

IN BERKELEY COUNTY, twenty-two rifle shots from R. C. Butler's farm, was a house said to be haunted. It was known as the West Fogle house.

One spring, on the first day of April, the Fogles moved

out. The men started early in the morning with the lighter loads, leaving the heavier loads for later. Mrs. Fogle and her infant child were to go last of all. Having some time on her hands, Mrs. Fogle sat down in her old rocking chair and started rocking her baby.

An old dog wandered in and lay down on the hearth. All at once a miracle took place in front of the woman's eyes. The dog changed into a man! He held up one hand and in a soft voice begged her not to be frightened.

He told her he knew she was brave enough to follow his instructions. He pointed out a secluded spot where he had buried a few thousand dollars, and insisted she take it for future use. He said he had tried again and again to tell other tenants where the money was, but when the transformation would take place, each person would run away. The woman took the money, and the house was haunted no more.

45. Aunt Betsy Barr and Her Dog

DURING WORLD WAR I, a bad flu epidemic swept the little community of Sedalia. There was an old maiden woman who had lived alone, except for a little white dog, since the death of her parents. Every family was down sick, so no one had any time to pay any attention to old Aunt Betsy Barr for a few days. Finally a neighbor who lived about a mile up the valley called his wife's attention to the fact that no smoke was coming out of Aunt Betsy's chimney. Even though he was just up from a sickbed himself, he went out and hitched the horses to the sled, and drove down with his son.

He found the door latched and no tracks in the snow, which had fallen a few days before. He pounded on the door and rapped on the windows. There was no answer, not even a bark from the dog. He told his boy he believed something was wrong, and he guessed they had better break the door open.

They found old Betsy in bed, and the dog stretched out before the fireplace, stiff and cold. They had been dead for days. The man sent for help with the bodies, and after a day or so, the woman and dog were buried.

A few weeks later this same man went to town to the mill. He was gone longer than he expected, and it was dark before he got home. As he passed Aunt Betsy's place, he heard a dog whine. Turning around, he saw Aunt Betsy and her dog, both sitting on the back end of his sled. He realized they must have been there since he passed the cemetery, away back down the road, where the horses had shied and broken into a trot.

She said, "Don't be worried, Oliver. You came and straightened out my bones and put me away right. Now, I have come to tell you something. Under a loose hearth stone you will find my gold. Take it and keep it for you and Mandy. You were always the ones who helped me."

Oliver finally found breath to speak, to tell her how sorry he was because they had not come sooner, but she and the dog were gone. They disappeared before his eyes. He whipped up the horses and hurried home.

The next day Oliver, Mandy, and the boy went down to Aunt Betsy's house. They found the loose hearth stone, and sure enough, under it was the gold in an old, black, snap pocketbook. Each piece was wrapped separately in tissue paper and crowded into the pocketbook. It amounted to several hundred dollars.

46. The Ghost Girl

THREE YEARS AGO John Huffman's son Ward and his family were living in a small house in the Bunner's Ridge section.

One night they decided to go to town and hired a young girl to stay at the house until they returned. They had been gone about an hour when the girl heard a knock and opened the door. There stood a stranger, who asked her for some food or money.

Mr. Huffman didn't believe much in banks and kept his money in the house. The girl was scared, but she went to get some food. As she went through the house, she slipped the money through a crack in the floor.

The stranger, however, came into the house and demanded that the girl tell him where the money was. She wouldn't do it, and he killed her and ransacked the house. When they returned the Huffmans found the girl's body, but didn't find the money, and were certain they had been robbed.

The third night after the girl had been buried, something strange happened. About midnight they were suddenly awakened. There before them, at the exact place where the blood had been on the floor, was the girl they had hired. She remained a few seconds and vanished.

This went on a few nights, and Mr. Huffman decided to get a neighbor to sit up with him. The girl appeared as usual, and the neighbor noticed she was pointing to a spot on the floor. The floor board was pulled up and the money was found. After that, she never appeared again.

47. Aunt Bett's Ghost

BETT ENSINGER always kept her money hid in the house. One night, around midnight, some men came and pounded on the door, saying they were hungry and wanted a sandwich. She let them in and started to go and make sandwiches, but they said they didn't want anything to eat—they wanted her money. She said she didn't have any money. They killed her because they knew she was lying.

Bett didn't have any rugs on the floor, and the bloodstain wouldn't scrub off. The more you'd scrub, the brighter the stain would get. Every night after her funeral, she'd come back and would stand in the bedroom. Her folks told how she'd been coming back, standing in the room by the stain and then leaving when they didn't say anything.

One night a neighbor thought he'd come up and see if she really did come back—and she did. He was sitting in the room, and, as he looked up, there she was, looking at him. He asked her where her money was, because the family couldn't find it. She smiled and pointed at the blood stain and left again.

The next day they took the board up and found all her money under the stained spot. She was never seen again.

48. Hickory Nuts

THE OWNER OF an old brick house that was supposed to be haunted could get no one to live in it, so he offered a reward to anyone who would stay in it all night and prove that it was not haunted. Finally a young man agreed to do this.

About dusk he entered the house. In the bedroom was a large, open fireplace with a candle on the mantelpiece. He lit the candle, and then lit a fire from the wood already in the fireplace. The hearth was made of rough-hewn stone, about two by three feet in area.

Noticing a hammer and a bag of hickory nuts, he decided to crack some. After cracking a few of the nuts, he was astonished to see a human finger suddenly emerge from the seemingly solid rock, and then a whole hand. The light from the candle flickered and the fire in the fireplace seemed to burn more quietly. Knowing the thing would have to answer if asked a question in the name of the Creator, the man said, "What in the name of God do you want?"

"Raise this rock," said a voice, and the hand disappeared. The young man worked most of the night to remove the rock. Under it, in old coins, he found money enough to last him the rest of his life.

9   Haunted Places

CONSIDERED IN one way, stories of haunted houses and places are the most numerous of ghost stories, for one may think of any place where a ghost appears as being haunted. In the stories given here the existence of the haunting itself seemed more important than other elements of the tales. In "The Floating Coffin," for example, the main point is that a particular portion of a road is haunted, and in "The Old Burnt House" there are a variety of events related by the haunting of one particular house.

All collectors of ghost tales include haunted house stories, but some of the most unusual ones are in St. John D. Seymour and Harry L. Neligan's *True Irish Ghost Stories.* Newbell N. Puckett, in his *Folk Beliefs of the Southern Negro,* also gives some interesting examples of "Layin' de Sperrit," "Negro Ha'ants," and "Fightin' de Ghosses."

49. The Floating Coffin

Not long after the end of the Civil War, a Mrs. Hess Bender, who lived near Bobtown, which is near Monongah, was going home and stopped for a drink of water at the Smiths. Mrs. Smith met her at the door, told her supper was about ready, and asked her to come in and have supper with them. She did and then started on home.

She had been gone about half an hour when she came back to the Smiths. At first she claimed to have forgotten her bonnet and that she could not do without it. Then she told them that as she was going along, about the middle of the stretch of road that lay along the edge of the woods near the bank of Booth's Creek, where, as stories had it, a drawer from Pennsylvania had been murdered, she saw a coffin with a man sitting on it rise from the upper side of the road. It came up about as high as her head, went quartering across the road, and disappeared over the creek bank. She said she was scared and had come back to stay all night.

Later, Isaac Koon, an old farmer living a short distance away, saw the same thing. Then two women who lived near Bobtown saw the coffin and man. Several others reported that they had seen it, and it always came up from the same place on the upper side of the road, crossed the road, and went over the creek bank at the same place, and was always seen about the same time in the evening.

Several years afterward, some boys from Monongah and Rhea Chapel were at Boothsville playing baseball. A new road had been made up the creek, but the old road was still open. In the evening Tom Rhea, Barney Whaling, and Will Barnes were coming from the ball game on horseback and took the old road, for it was shorter to their homes. Tom was a few steps in front of Barney and Will.

Barney called to Tom and said, "Say, Tom, right along here some place is where that dead man lives."

71

"Yes," said Tom. "I wish I could see him. I would whistle for him to dance."

Just then the coffin and man came up from the side of the road. Tom's horse saw it, reared, and whirled to run. Tom was a good rider, or he would have been thrown. Barney and Will watched the coffin and man cross the road and disappear over the creek bank.

All of the old people living around there have passed on, and I have not heard a word about the man and coffin for more than fifty years.

50.   The Old Burnt House

BEFORE THE CIVIL War, near a community known now as Knob Fork, about seven miles from Littleton, a log house was built. The old log part consisted of three large rooms. In the end room and middle room were two large, open fireplaces. In later years an upper story was built.

Sometime during the Civil War a poor "boundary jumper"° on a horse made his way into the small community. Some of the people provided food and lodging for a few nights, for him and his horse. One day the horse was found roaming around, with the bridle and saddle still on, but the man was never seen or heard of again. And since it was near this old house where no one was living at the time that the horse had been found, some feared that he had been murdered and his body hidden nearby.

Soon after, people who were passing by the house in the evenings told of hearing screams and moans and other strange sounds. Often riders would have to get off and lead their horses until they were well past the house because the horses kept neighing and trying to turn back. If a dog

---

° This phrase probably refers to a southerner who, unsympathetic with the Confederate cause, came North to avoid having to fight for the Confederacy.

were along, it kept as close to its master as possible, whether he were riding or walking. Often horses would stop to drink from the stream that came down from the house and ran along the side of the road. When they walked into the ditch, the water seemed to turn red as they lifted their hoofs.

Later, when the Strawsburgh family purchased the farm and moved in, they heard strange noises during the day and evening, as if a body were being dragged across the floor of the upstairs.

One time a niece of Mrs. Strawsburgh was visiting her aunt, and a young fellow from around those parts was calling on her. As they sat in front of a blazing fire, the girl heard a clicking noise, and looking in the direction of the door, she saw that the latch was going up and down. She was so frightened she couldn't move at first, but when she did, she let out a scream and ran up the stairs and hid behind her aunt's bed. According to the family, the young man never did any more courting in that house.

Another time Mrs. Strawsburgh's mother came to spend the night with her daughter and slept in a room over the old log part. The next night her daughter asked her how she slept.

She said, "Fine, up until about twelve o'clock, when I woke up with the feeling that a cold hand was being passed over my face. Looking around, I could see a hand moving away into the shadows."

She had planned to stay the next night but was called home.

In addition to all these things, the Strawsburgh family were not able to keep the quilts on the beds at night. No matter how well or how often they pulled up the covers, they kept sliding to the foot. Also, there was a certain place on the floor in the back room downstairs that had the appearance of blood. And, in spite of all the scrubbing and scraping they did, they were never able to get rid of it.

Finally the Strawsburghs put the farm up for sale. There was one good point about owning this property, and that was it had a wonderful well of water. It had never been known to go dry. In those days that meant something to a Wetzel County farmer and his family.

Mr. D—'s father next bought the farm, against his family's wishes. They didn't move in right away, but put in some crops. Often, on coming to the place in late afternoon, they could hear moaning and sometimes something like a scream, but, on going into the house, would find no one.

One time the two older boys went into the house to nail up the door that led from the large middle room downstairs into the log shop and refused to stay shut. They took a large plank and nailed it with spike nails. They thought surely they would never have any more trouble with it and turned to leave. Just before they reached the door leading to the outside, they heard the sound of splitting wood, and looking back into the room, they saw the plank board had split right down the middle. The door was slowly swinging open.

Late that spring, the D— family moved into the house, the father assuring them it was all a lot of nonsense about the noises and the idea of the house being haunted. One evening, while in the front room, they heard sounds as if a lot of chickens were fluttering underneath the hearth. That happened so many times that the father, in the fall, consented to let the two older brothers take up the fireplace, but they found nothing but a straight razor.

One night, while everyone was sitting out on the side porch, or a little place where the roof went out over the well, there was a sound like a shot, and the bullet seemed to whiz past and bounce down into the water in the well.

Often in the night, when the family were upstairs sleeping, they would be awakened by a crashing sound, as if every dish in the kitchen cupboard had fallen to the floor, but they would find everything in order—the dishes just as they had been put away, not one broken. The two older brothers made the log room in the back into a blacksmith shop, and some days they couldn't keep the bellows going at all.

Some lady, who had known about the boundary jumper's disappearance, told the D—'s that if they would take up the fireplace in the back log room, they would have no more trouble. They did and found a pair of old boots. Sometimes, the two brothers heard a sound like the dropping of money and would stoop to pick it up, but there would be none.

The father took sick and died, and the family got rid of the farm. Later a large pipe line went through this farm, and while some of the laborers camped on a part of it, the house caught fire and all of it burned but the back room and the chimney.

Even then people still told of the queer sounds they could hear as they went by, and for many years it was known as the Old Burnt House.

Sometime later, someone put in a field of crops on the place and dug the old foundation up. Some said they found an old daybook, but it was so old and rotten, no one could read it. After this, the ghost never came back, so far as Mr. D— knew.

51.   A Skeleton Hand

THERE WAS A family living at Archie Fork that thought their house was haunted. The man said whenever he went anywhere after dark, it seemed as if there were someone walking behind him. After a while he decided to move because this made him very nervous.

On the night before the family was to move, the man told his wife he was hungry and would like something to eat before going to bed. She told him there was a pie in

the kitchen. He went to the kitchen, got the pie, and had just started to pick up the knife, when a bony, white hand took the knife, cut a piece of pie, and left with it.

He got his family together and left that night and not a person has moved there since.

52. The Upstairs Bedroom

MR. AND MRS. George Sype bought an old house in the country for a very reasonable sum. The house had the reputation of being haunted, and no one would live there. Years before, in the only upstairs bedroom, a woman was murdered by having her throat slit with a straight razor while she was asleep.

Mr. and Mrs. Sype moved into their new home. Everything went well, and the murder room was only used as a spare bedroom. Several months later, a huckster, passing through the neighborhood, stopped late one night and wanted to spend the night. Mr. Sype showed their guest to the spare room and they all retired for the night. He was reassuring his wife that all the stories about the room were false, when they heard a loud scream. Their guest came down the stairs two at a time.

The huckster stated that he soon fell asleep, but was awakened by a whetting noise. Rising up in bed, he saw a woman in a nightdress coming toward him with a shaving mug, whetting a long straight razor. He thought he was dreaming, but she came closer and began to place lather on his neck. As she drew back to use the razor, he leaped from the bed and rushed downstairs to find his hosts. His nightclothes and his neck were wet, and Mrs. Sype insisted she saw traces of lather.

Mr. and Mrs. Sype lived on for many years in this house. They never again were bothered with the walking ghost, but then they never again used the upstairs spare bedroom.

53. *Anna Conrad*

ON THE EDGE of Grant Town there stands an old, fourteen-room house, which nobody has lived in since 1946. The house looks like any other old, empty house, but this one has a story behind it.

The house was the home of Burt Conrad and his family of ten children. In March of 1936, Anna Conrad, one of the children, was badly burned on her face, chest, and both legs. She spent nine months in a Pittsburgh hospital. After she returned home, everybody was nice to her, but in a few months her brothers and sisters began to ignore her because she was a cripple and her face was ugly. She knew that they were tired of her, so she moved her bedroom to one of the back rooms on the top floor. She had her meals brought up to her.

She never left her room for eight months, and then one night she decided to go downstairs. On her way down the second flight of stairs, she fell and hit her head.

When she had recovered the next day, she kept saying, "I have to go with her."

Her parents couldn't understand what she was talking about, but when they looked out the window, they saw the footprints of a woman in the snow. And when they followed the prints, they found they led uphill to the family graveyard and stopped over Burt Conrad's first wife's grave.

The parents were worried, and they locked Anna in her room. Then she became insane. She would scream and laugh at the same time.

One cold March night Anna took a fit, tore the door off

its hinges, and started on a mad prowl through the house, breaking everything in sight. Her father grabbed her, but she broke his arm to free herself. She had acquired supernatural strength from somewhere. Then she returned to her room, and in a little while the frightened family heard her scream.

When they got up to the room, they found Anna hanging by her neck from the light cord. She had killed herself. After this, both of the parents also lost their minds.

Even today, people near the empty house on a windy March night can hear Anna's last scream. And nobody will live in the house because of Anna's screaming.

54. *Wizard's Clipp*

ABOUT TWELVE miles south of Shepherdstown and seven miles west of Charlestown is a little town called Middleway, sometimes called Smithfield, and often called Clipp. In it lived Adam Livingston, who had come from Lancaster, Pennsylvania, about 1790, and had purchased a small farm. About four years later, a stranger of middle age and respectable appearance arrived and was received as a boarder in the Livingston home. In a few days the stranger became very ill. He asked Livingston to find a Catholic priest for him, but Livingston refused. The stranger died. His name was unknown. There was nothing among his effects to show anything of his history.

On the night of the death, a man was asked to sit up with the corpse. Queer things happened—lights went out and footstep sounds were heard. The members of the household were thoroughly frightened. In a few days matters became worse. The sound of horses' galloping around the house at night was heard. Livingston's barn was burned, and his cattle died. Dishes were thrown upon the floor. Money disappeared. The heads of chickens and turkeys dropped off. Burning chunks of wood leaped from the fireplace, endangering the house.

Soon the annoyances, which were destroying Adam Livingston's peace of mind, assumed a new form. The sound of shears was heard in his house, and his blankets, sheets, and counterpanes, his boots, saddle, and clothing were clipped in half moons and other curious figures. This continued for three months.

People for thirty miles around gathered to see and hear. One old lady testified that before entering the house, she took off her good black silk cap and wrapped it in a handkerchief to protect it. When she left the house, she unwrapped the cap and found it cut into ribbons. Three young men from Winchester, Virginia, came to spend the night "and to face the devil himself if he were the author of these things," but as soon as they were comfortably seated, a large stone leaped from the fireplace and whirled around the floor. The young men took to their heels and escaped.

By this time poor Livingston was almost insane. He appealed to three professed conjurers, but their incantations were in vain. Soon he had a dream in which he saw a man "in robes" and heard a voice saying, "This is the man who can help you." After many inquiries and much searching, he was led to come to the Catholic Church in Shepherdstown. When the priest appeared at the altar, he proved to be the man in the dream.

When he heard the remarkable story, the priest, Father Dennis Cohill, laughed at it and said probably some of the neighbors were plaguing him, and he must keep a watch for them.

Mr. Livingston pleaded with tears for help. Father Cohill went to the house, sprinkled it with holy water, received a gift of money, and finally had mass celebrated in the house. This proved effective, and the ghostly visitation ceased.

Mr. Livingston returned to Pennsylvania, but before doing so, he conveyed the Clipp property to trustees for the benefit of the Catholic Church.

55. Vinegar Hill

ABOUT THE time of the settling of Benton's Ferry, on top of Vinegar Hill, near the Vincent cemetery, lived several brothers. Down the river a little way was a large brick inn, used as a way station by railroadmen and cattlemen. When the old inn was filled to capacity, the spirits flowed freely, and the merrymaking could be heard all along the river on a still summer evening. The brothers, who lived on the hill, specialized in making cider vinegar, which some of the cattlemen would deliver for them when they drove a herd of cattle through to the eastern markets.

One night, during a heavy thunderstorm, as one of the brothers was going down the hill with a wagonload of barrels, the old mule stopped suddenly and the topmost barrel rolled off onto the driver, pinning him to the ground. His howls and groans soon brought his brothers to his aid, and as they had been sampling the vinegar quite frequently that day, they were feeling good. Instead of lifting the barrel off, they just gave it a push and let it roll. The poor man was mashed twice as long and wide as before and, of course, soon went to his final resting place in the old graveyard.

Since that time, on dark stormy nights, when the thunder rolled and rumbled around the hill, anyone who happened to be caught walking up the road, would see first two large, black spots that looked like eyes, and then very slowly a cloud of white mist would arise from the road and surround the spots. Then, with a cackling sound, the mist would take the form of a huge flat man, who would beckon the person to follow, all the time staggering about, sometimes falling and sometimes dancing along in front, screaming like a banshee and clapping its flattened hands until it reached the top of the hill. There, with the accompaniment of a sound like hundreds of barrels rolling down the hill, it would give one last cackle and disappear in the grave-yard.

After the death of the brothers, there was no more vinegar made on the hill, and the merrymaking at the inn ceased.

56. *The Living Corpse*

ONE NIGHT early in the Civil War a wagonload of wounded soldiers was camped on the edge of the small town of Pennsboro, waiting for a doctor and supplies to catch up with them. The following morning, one of the soldiers had apparently died and was taken to the local undertaker to be prepared for burial. Because this was a busy day for the undertaker, the body was placed in a tub of ice water to preserve it until it could be embalmed.

Early the next morning, the actual embalming was begun. The first thing that was done was to sew the corpse's mouth shut from the inside. Next a needle and tube were attached to each arm so that the embalming fluid could be pumped into one arm while the blood was drained from the other.

This process had no sooner begun when the man sat up. The people present could see the man's mouth trying to work and opening to the limits of the stitches. The tubes were quickly yanked from his arms, but by this time it was too late because the embalming fluid had reached his heart. The man slowly settled back upon the table as if accepting his fate.

Shortly after this, many strange things began to happen at the undertaker's shop. Furniture would be rearranged and bodies moved. But the strangest thing of all was that no matter where embalming fluid and needles would be hid, the next morning the needles would be bent and the fluid spilled over the floor or missing.

Some people in the community thought this was the work of practical jokers, but others were not so sure. It did not matter to the undertaker, for within a year he was insane, with only memories of a happy childhood.

57. Old Gopher

ABOUT 1890, John Sweeney, a prosperous cattle buyer and owner of one of the biggest farms in the northwestern Shinnston area, lived in a large two-story brick house in Shinnston.

One day he heard of some fine cattle in the lower part of West Virginia for sale at a very reasonable price, and taking some money from the bank, he set out to buy them. He had told all his friends where he was going, so the whole town of Shinnston and the outlying communities knew of the proposed trip. What they did not know was the amount of money he would have with him.

Mr. Sweeney started on his trip about the first week in March. Ordinarily, he should have been back in about two weeks or a month at the most. When he had not returned in about six weeks, his friends began to worry about him. They wrote letters to the stockyard where he was to buy the cattle. About a week later a letter arrived at the mayor's office in Shinnston saying that no one at the stockyard had ever seen Mr. Sweeney.

This news shocked the whole area. What could have happened?

On the thirtieth of April a strange occurrence was reported. Ben Ashcraft said he was driving his team of horses across a stream that went through the Sweeney place. When he got in the middle of the bridge, a black figure tried to stop his wagon. The figure jumped on the wagon as the horses fled. It told Mr. Ashcraft that it would not rest until the day that Mr. Sweeney's murderer was drowned in the stream. It then disappeared.

From then on, the same thing happened to every man that went over the bridge. Whenever young boys would cross this bridge, they would not be able to eat for two or three days, if they had seen "Old Gopher," as the ghost was called.

These were not the only mysterious things to happen. Strange things were seen at the Sweeney house. Cows would sail around the house. Old Gopher and a witch would fly about in the trees. Men would walk in line, carrying their heads in their hands. Books would move from one table to another in the library. A man with a knife in his heart and a chain around his neck would lie in a chair screaming. No fire or even a pipe could be lighted on this property.

Everytime anyone would attempt to set foot on the bridge, he would see Old Gopher crying in the middle of it.

One day a man who had never been seen by anyone in the area was found drowned in the stream. Around his neck were wounds like those that might be left by a vampire. That same day the Sweeney place mysteriously burned down. The fire destroyed the entire farm, although it never so much as burned a blade of grass on neighboring farms. Old Gopher had avenged his murder as he said he would.

58. *The Ghost of Gamble's Run*

JOHN GAMBLE moved to Wetzel County in 1850. That fall he harvested a large crop of apples and made several barrels of cider. On his thirty-sixth birthday he started to

New Martinsville to obtain additional barrels for his cider, but he never returned.

He held a note for twenty dollars from the Whiteman brothers, to whom he had sold a wagon. On his way home he stopped at their house and asked if they wanted to cash the note, but learned they were not ready to pay it off.

Leb Mercer was also at the Whiteman home and Gamble owed him two dollars, the balance due on a calf. Mercer requested his two dollars, and Gamble drew a five-dollar bill from his pocket and asked Mercer if he could change it.

"No," replied Mercer, "I can't change it. Is that all you have?"

"No," Gamble answered. "I have almost two hundred dollars and nothing smaller than a five. Stop by my house in a few days and I will pay you."

It was getting dark, and Gamble started home. Mercer left shortly afterward. Gamble got in his skiff and started rowing upstream. About two o'clock that night Mercer was seen around New Martinsville, his clothing wet. The next day Gamble was found, murdered and robbed, his body lying near the stream and his skiff overturned.

Suspicion pointed to Leb Mercer as the murderer, but he said he was innocent and came up with an alibi for the period after he left the Whiteman home. He was never arrested but was watched to see if he seemed to have more money than usual.

Later that fall there was a cornhusking on Point Pleasant Ridge near New Martinsville, and a number of young people went, among them a John Hindman. On their way home, several of the young men decided to take different routes to see who could reach the town first. Hindman chose to go over a hill, coming down on what is now called Gamble's Run.

As he walked along the creek bank near the river, the form of a man appeared before him and called out, "I am John Gamble. I was killed by Leb Mercer. Take him in and have justice done." Then the figure was gone as suddenly as it had appeared.

Hindman became frightened and ran into town. He told the story of what he had seen and heard. At first the people refused to believe it, but young Hindman described the ghost. His description agreed with the personal appearance of John Gamble, and young Hindman had never seen Gamble.

Feeling ran high. Leb Mercer was arrested and brought to trial on a charge of first-degree murder. He secured a lawyer who finally succeeded in convincing the jury that "ghost evidence" could not be accepted in a court of law. Many people said the lawyer had difficulty in keeping Mercer from confessing after the trial got under way, but he won the case and set the man free. Guilty or not, Mercer experienced an ordeal—haunted by a ghost, hounded by the law, and accused by his former friends of being a murderer. He moved to St. Mary's, where it was reported that he acted strangely, talking and muttering to himself, until his death.

10   Negro Slaves

I‍T MAY BE that the tales in this group represent a category that is slowly disappearing, since the institution which created it no longer exists. Or it may be that these unfortunate souls are so bitter that their spirits may wander for a long time yet. I had thought there were few such stories left, although I realized that in the days of slavery and immediately afterward there must have been many of them, but I keep getting new ones.

The ghosts of these tales, except for the glowing eyes of Kettle Run and possibly the saddle ghost, seem prompted by a desire for retribution; at least, they all have some grievance at their deaths. One might speculate whether there were tales of well-disposed slave spirits who returned to show their appreciation for some special kindness of their masters.

Geographically, ghosts of this type are found throughout the eastern United States. Louis C. Jones reports them from New York and John Harden from North Carolina, and Helen Creighton in *Bluenose Ghosts* has an especially vivid tale of the ghost of a child slave.

59. *The Tombstone*

MY STORY about a cruel slaveowner was related to my grandfather by his father. My grandfather was a good friend of the slaveowner's son and told me that the son always had large groups of men working, literally at nothing, and that he paid them large salaries. The son said that his father had cheated people out of money all his life, and he, the son, was just trying to pay some of it back.

As the story goes, one day. Mr. Soames, the slaveowner, was inspecting one of his favorite plots of ground. An old Negro had been told to hoe a potato patch in that part of the estate, but instead he was sitting in the shade of a tree. Upon seeing this, the owner flew into a rage and beat the old man to death with the hoe. Two years later the slaveowner fell dead on the exact spot where he had killed the Negro. Two local doctors could not find any cause for his death, and as far as anyone knew, he was in perfect health. HERE LIES MR. SOAMES was all that was put on his tombstone.

Some three or four months later a young boy happened to be passing the grave at night and heard a sound like someone using a chisel. The boy could see no one at the tombstone or near it. He reported the incident to the son, and the son looked at the tombstone the next morning.

A much larger epitaph had been chiseled into the rock. Below HERE LIES MR. SOAMES were now the following lines:

> He stole from the poor;
> He robbed from the rich;

Gone to hell,
The son of a b——.

60. How Kettle Run Was Named

ABOUT A HALF mile above the Benton's Ferry Bridge, at the
foot of Vinegar Hill, stands an old log house called "The
Log." A deep gully named Kettle Run reaches from Route
250 to the Tygart Valley River. At this point is another
gully on the north side of the river, directly across from
"The Log," called Copper Hollow.

Now, I have been told that on a still, dark night, from a
window overlooking the river, one could see pairs of small,
bright lights marching down Copper Hollow to the river,
where they would cross over and disappear up Kettle Run.
All the while there would be heard a mournful chanting.

It is said that during the Civil War, the Yankees
brought slaves down the gully, hid them in "The Log," and
crossed the river there instead of at the old ferry. Then
the slaves would follow Copper Hollow north to freedom.

One night while a dozen or more slaves were waiting
for safe passage down Kettle Run, a band of raiders found
them. After killing them, the raiders cut off their heads,
put them in a large, copper kettle, and carried them to the
river bank. There they left them while they went back for
the bodies.

The family living at "The Log" took the kettle of heads
across the river and up Copper Hollow to the old Linn
Cemetery and buried them in a long, narrow grave. Since
that time the heads have been trying to find their bodies,
and it is the eyes of the murdered slaves that can be seen
coming down the hollow and crossing the river. But only
people living in "The Log" could see the lights, and only
from the small window overlooking the river.

"The Log" still stands, but it has been remodeled and the window removed. And the lights are no longer seen.

61. The Cruel Slave Master

A NEGRO SLAVE, who was nearly seven feet tall, was killed by his cruel master because he was supposed to have stolen some money. Right after the Negro's death, strange things started to happen to the slaveowner who had killed him. Some of his slaves got sick and died. The rest of them ran away. His house burned down, and he lost all of his money. His wife left him. All of this happened within ten months of the time he killed the Negro. And during these months the tall ghost of the slave was seen walking over his land.

Now the master began to be frightened because the Negro had said, as he was dying, that he would take revenge for his death within the next year, and in exactly one year, he would kill the master.

It happened as the slave had foretold it. At about midnight people were awakened by screams from the slaveowner's house, and when they rushed to see what was happening, they saw the big Negro's ghost dragging away the screaming master. The people were too frightened to do anything but watch as the ghost dragged the master out of sight. Neither the ghost nor the master was ever seen afterward.

62. The Unusual Saddle

IN 1930 MY grandfather was spending the night alone in his home, which was surrounded by woodland and set off the main road about a quarter of a mile.

Since the weather was warm, he decided that he would sleep on the back porch. After he was finally resting comfortably, he became aware of a noise coming from the attic, a noise like slow footsteps. My grandfather, thinking that it was just the steps creaking, ignored it. A few minutes later he realized that the noise was approaching the bottom floor of the house. He lay there too frightened to move.

He lay still for what seemed hours. Finally the noise reached the back porch. Slowly the door opened and a large black shadow came out onto the porch. This shadow stood wavering over him for a number of minutes and then left the house completely.

The next morning my grandfather looked about the attic. He found a very odd-colored dark saddle. He examined the saddle but could not remember anything about it. Puzzled, he took it to an expert leather craftsman.

The leather craftsman studied the saddle, and after some time he found a diary hidden inside the covering. The diary had belonged to my great-great-grandfather.

It revealed that my great-great-grandfather had owned a slave who was horrified by horses. Because of this fear, the master had hated the slave, and when the slave died, he had had him skinned, and used the skin to cover the unusual saddle.

11 Murdered Peddlers

WEST VIRGINIA is unusually rich in tales of murdered peddlers and in the ghosts of these unfortunate men. Though only four selections are included here, I have collected more stories in this category than in any other.

Traveling alone with all his goods on his back through miles and miles of hill-and-valley wilderness and being one of few persons in the countryside with a supply of ready money, the peddler offered a ready victim to men's avarice. It was not always in the most isolated regions, though, that he was murdered; many were reportedly killed in the vicinity of Fairmont. Most of the murderers apparently went scot-free, and many a local fortune may have had its beginning in the death of a wandering peddler.

These unfortunate peddlers must have been gentle men, for their ghosts are generally not malevolent, being content usually to appear as melancholy memorials of their deaths.

The murdered peddler is a common figure in American folklore, and other collections, such as Louis C. Jones' *Things That Go Bump in the Night*, Vance Randolph's *Ozark Superstitions*, and E. E. Gardner's *Folklore from the Schoharie Hills*, contain a number of examples of the type.

63. A Ball of Fire

NO ONE NOTICED when the old peddler rode toward the residence of his bachelor friend. This was his third month in Glenville, and the neighbors were used to seeing him go one day and return a week later.

This evening he was tired, nervous, and wanted a shave, so he asked his friend to shave him. The bachelor agreed, and began preparing for the task. He lathered the peddler's face, stropped the razor, and began shaving him. The bachelor was hard-pressed for cash, and knowing the peddler carried a rather large sum of money, he decided to take advantage of circumstances, and cut his throat, then and there. Then he cut the body into several parts and, taking them into the garden, buried them in the hotbed. He turned the horse loose, headed it out of town, and hoped it would wander far off.

The bachelor searched the peddler's clothing and rifled the baggage, taking the money and some of the jewelry. The remainder he burned or buried. Before burying the body, he removed a ring from the peddler's finger.

Afraid that stray dogs might smell the buried body and dig it up, he went out a couple of nights later, dug up the body, put the pieces in a sack, and went to the river late at night. Coming to a whirlpool, he put rocks in the sack, tied it, and tossed it into the pool. In his haste he forgot to dig up the head to the body.

About five months later, a circuit judge, in town to hold

court, rode down the road by the river. When he came within two hundred yards of the whirlpool, he saw a ball of fire above the road.

The judge could not imagine what caused such a thing, so he stopped the horse when he came to the spot where the ball of fire was. To his amazement, the ball of fire changed form and became a headless man. This headless man got into the judge's buggy and told him the whole story of his death, and the circumstances connected with it. He wanted the judge to indict the bachelor on a charge of murder.

The judge, however, afraid people would think him insane for bringing a case before the court without a corpse or evidence, let the matter drop. He did, however, make inquiries. The only information to come forth was that the bachelor was seen wearing the peddler's ring and had acquired about two thousand dollars several months before. No one knew what had happened to the peddler.

64. The Murdered Merchant's Ghost

IN A RURAL section of Wirt County, before the Civil War, a merchant, traveling toward home after his day's work, was murdered and robbed. His head was completely severed from his body by a shotgun blast at close range, and his horses and wagon tied to a tree.

The Low Gap, as the place where the murder occurred was known, immediately became a place of horror for night travelers. The ghost that appeared when people passed the place took on various forms.

According to one traveler, as he approached the spot,

a very large, doglike animal, or form, was lying in the road. He became frightened and yelled at the animal, but it did not move. He then picked up a stone and threw at it. Immediately the animal arose and floated through the air down over the Low Gap and disappeared.

Two men, who were passing the place by night, told of a large ball of fire that came down the hill, touching the tree tops and making a hissing sound. It crossed the highway, and it too disappeared over the Low Gap.

On another night a traveler was walking along the highway in front of the Low Gap, when he saw what appeared to be a man coming toward him, carrying a lantern. Just as the man got almost to him, the lantern's light vanished.

The traveler, who was almost too frightened to talk, said, "What's the matter? Did your light go out?"

A coarse voice slowly replied, "No, my life went out."

Immediately a white, ghostlike form arose from the spot where the lantern was last seen and floated in the air to vanish over the Low Gap.

A prominent jeweler, who did not believe any of the stories he had heard about the merchant's ghost, decided to prove his disbelief by walking by the place alone one dark night. When he came back to his friends, they noticed he was very pale and did not care to talk. Upon being questioned, however, he told of seeing a headless man as he approached the place. When he got almost to the form, it crossed the highway and started floating through the air till it too vanished over the Low Gap.

Everyone also knew the story of the lone pedestrian, who, on approaching the haunted place, heard weird screams. When he shined a light in the direction of the sounds, he saw a nude man with blood on his face running wildly to the usual spot. Like the other apparitions, he too vanished and the screaming stopped just as abruptly.

Many persons of Wirt County are still fearful of passing Low Gap at night.

65. Strange Noises

THIS INCIDENT happened during the latter part of the nineteenth century in Grant County. During this time there were a great number of traveling salesmen, and many of them were robbed and killed for their money. As a precaution, the salesmen tried to travel in pairs, staying the night at two different places. They could then check on each other the next morning, and if anything happened to either one of them, the other could report it to the authorities.

Late one evening two travelers stopped at an inn. One of them was a cattleman and the other, a peddler. The cattleman stayed at the inn, and the peddler went to the nearest farmhouse to spend the night. The next morning the peddler went to the inn and asked the keeper if the cattleman was up and about yet. When the innkeeper told the peddler that he did not know anything about the cattleman, the peddler was sure that something had happened to him. In fact he was almost sure the cattleman had been killed, so he reported the incident to the authorities. When investigation was made, nothing could be proved against the innkeeper, and he was freed of the charge.

Within the next few years the innkeeper became very ill. He was so ill that he was more dead than alive. He was in this condition for a long time, and it seemed as if he just kept hanging on to what little life was left in him. One day he told the doctor that he wanted to make a confession. He told the doctor about the night the cattleman had stayed at his inn. During the night while the cattleman was sleeping, he had sneaked into his room and stabbed him to death and then dragged him outside and thrown him over a cliff. He had hoped to rob him of a large sum of money, but the cattleman only had $1.00 on him at the time. As soon as the innkeeper had made his confession, he died.

A couple of years later my great-uncle, who had a job close by, stayed at this same inn. His room was next to the one where the cattleman had been murdered. For several nights, at around nine o'clock, he would hear a noise. It sounded like someone dropping a bag of feed; after it hit the floor, it would be dragged out to the top of the stairs. One night he decided he would go out in the hall and see what it was. As soon as he went into the hall, the noise stopped and he did not see anything. After this last experience, he did not stay there any longer.

All the people who lived close by said the place was haunted. Finally the owner left, and it burned down. Even after it had burned, people used to come from far and near to hear the strange noises.

66. The Tin Cup

JOHN MASON was a newcomer to the little settlement at Bigbend in Calhoun County. He bought a small tract of land just below the village and built a small cabin. The man's past was a mystery. No one knew where he came from, and for a time he was the subject of much speculation in the village.

If John Mason was disturbed by the speculation, he did not show it. He soon found his place in the community. His attendance at church seemed to justify him in the eyes of his fellow men, and they did not ask him questions about his past. He had no family and no relatives in the vicinity.

Soon the men in the village began to drop by his cabin to visit. They swapped stories and invited him to join them on their coon hunts.

One night, in late fall, John Mason accompanied a party of coon hunters. The chase led the party across

Bigbend Creek and in the vicinity of Mason's cabin. While crossing the creek, one of the hunters slipped on a log and fell into the cold water. It was quite cold, and the party went to Mason's cabin for the man to dry out his clothing.

As they sat in the cabin waiting for their friend to dry, they fell to telling stories. Mason was a genial host and poured each man a cup of cider. Soon the conversation turned to one of the mysteries of that area—what had happened to Sam Conners, the old peddler who had made regular rounds, carrying his goods and wares in a pack.

"Did you know Sam Conners, John?" asked Jim Davis.

"I'm afraid not," replied Mason.

"I thought maybe you did because of these cups. We have some at home like them that my wife bought from old Sam."

"No, I bought these at a sale somewhere."

The talk turned to other matters. The men decided to call off the hunt and go home. About that time one of the coon hounds outside began to wail mournfully. Then another long, mournful wail came from the dogs outside.

The hunters fell silent for a few moments. Each could recognize his dog's voice, and although they appeared to pass off the wailing lightly, each regarded it as an omen of some impending disaster or perhaps even a death in the owner's family.

The hunters gazed at each other in silence and were startled as the floor boards of John Mason's cabin creaked and the door opened.

"Who is it?" called out Jim Davis, sharply.

"It must have been the wind," said Mason.

Davis stood up and went to the door. There was no wind. The dogs wailed again. He opened the door and spoke softly to them, and the wailing stopped. He sat down and, looking at the wet hunter, suggested they go home if he were dry.

Again the floor boards creaked near the door. The men

looked at each other. No one had moved. They looked at Mason.

"I guess I didn't get the foundation deep enough," said Mason. "The freezing ground must be pushing up the floor."

The hunters gathered up their guns and lanterns, said good night, and departed with their dogs. It was cold, but the ground was not freezing. On the way home, Davis suggested the men get together and help Mason fix his floor and door the next day.

The men agreed and met at the Mason cabin the next morning with their tools. When they explained to Mason that they wanted to help him fix the foundation of his cabin, he said he had planned to go to town on urgent business. His friends told him to go ahead and assured him that when he returned the job would be done.

Mason went back into his cabin, procured a large pouch which he dropped in his coat pocket, and set out for town after thanking the men for their kindness.

Davis and the others set to work digging out the stone foundation on either side of the cabin door. The ground had not yet frozen and the digging was not difficult. A sudden clink caused Jim Davis to withdraw his mattock quickly. He reached down and drew out a small tin saucer.

"Look," he said, "one of old Sam Conner's saucers."

The others crowded in close. Silently, with pale faces, they shoveled dirt. In a few minutes they pulled out the old peddler's pack, rotted from the damp earth. Under it lay his skeleton, both arms extended and the hands pushing upward, as if to push off the weight of his earthen grave.

The mystery was solved. Old Sam had been murdered and robbed. He always carried large sums of money in a leather pouch, confident that no harm would befall him because he was loved by all who knew him.

It was now clear. John Mason had beaten the old peddler and robbed him of his money. It appeared that the old man had been buried before he was quite dead, and still had the strength to extend his arms upward in an effort to raise up from his grave.

The story of the old peddler was told for many years and the character of his murderer discussed. When John Mason was captured as he fled from the county, he was still carrying old Sam's moneypouch.

12 Mine Ghosts

THERE HAVE been hundreds of mine accidents in West Virginia, with undoubtedly many more victims—nearly four hundred were killed in one accident alone—and the dark passageways of the coal mines are indeed likely places for ghosts and visitations. Perhaps it is no wonder then that there are so many wandering ghosts of miners. By and large they are friendly souls—neither violent nor malevolent—like Big John and Jeremy Walker, who come back to see how things are getting along and to lend a helping hand when needed. Sometimes there is an element of protest—one man wants to make sure that the mine officials give his widow what is justly hers—but in none of the tales I have collected which take place in the mines is there an element of retribution.

The Grant Town mine, the scene of four of the stories

here, is one of the largest in the United States, and possibly in the world. The town itself, with a population of a little over a thousand, is about seven miles northwest of Fairmont. Surrounded by hills, it is a kind of sunken garden— a well at the bottom of the stairway of hills and highways —so that it seems to be in a world of its own. In a way, perhaps, it is. At least fourteen different European nationalities live in the town and work in the mine.

67. Big John's Ghost

MY GRANDFATHER was a coal miner all of his life. He had started to work in the coal mines of Wales when he was only eleven years old. He told me many of his experiences in the mines, some of which I found quite hard to believe.

One story I remember very well was about a big Russian coal miner and an accident which took place when the Grant Town mine was just getting its start. Grandfather said they called this man Big John because he was such a huge man. Big John loved to work and he loved to talk while he worked.

Grandfather worked with Big John all day. John planted the charges to blow the coal out, and Grandfather fixed the plunger. One day John was planting the dynamite in a vein of coal and Grandfather was around the corner, fixing the plunger that detonated the charge. All of a sudden he heard an explosion and a terrible scream. He ran around the corner to find Big John lying on the ground, with his head completely blown off. A stick of dynamite had accidentally gone off.

It was a terrible shock to Grandfather, for he and John had become close friends while they worked together. It seemed as if he could still hear John talking while they

were going down in the cage, and while they worked. Now he was gone.

One foggy morning, about a month after the accident, Grandfather was going down in the cage by himself. All of a sudden he felt as if he were not alone. He slowly turned around. There before his eyes stood Big John, holding his head on his arm. The head smiled and spoke to Grandfather just as it used to do when it was on Big John's shoulders. Grandfather shut his eyes and kept them shut until the cage hit bottom. When he opened them, Big John was gone.

To this day Grandfather will get a funny look in his eyes when he tells this story. He will swear that he actually saw Big John. Who am I to doubt his word?

68. The Pointing Finger

IF YOU HAVE ever been in the coal mines, you know how troublesome sulfur balls are to the miners. Sulfur balls range from the size of a basketball to one ·weighing several tons, and whether large or small, they are almost impossible to drill. Jim Tokash, a "Joy" operator° in Section North Butt, thought he was the best coalcutter in the Grant Town coal mine. Whenever he ran into a vein of sulfur, instead of reporting it to the section boss, he would try to drill through it. He was warned many times by the section boss that if he didn't stop breaking the drill bits he would be fired.

One afternoon Jim ran into the biggest sulfur ball he had ever seen, and as before, he tried to drill through it.

° The Joy Manufacturing Company is one of the largest manufacturers of coal mining equipment. Here the machine is a coalcutter.

Jim drilled for about five minutes before the drill stopped. He got a crowbar and tried to pry the bit loose from the sulfur ball. All at once the drill broke loose in Jim's hand. The next thing he remembered, he was in a hospital. He looked down and discovered that his left hand was missing.

A few months later Jim returned to the mines—not as a Joy operator, but as an assistant. The new Joy operator also thought that he was the best coalcutter in the mines, and when he tried the same thing that Jim had, he caused a cave-in.

Jim Tokash was getting a drink of water at the time of the cave-in, and he was the only man alive in the section. He tried to get the men out from beneath the slate and coal, but it was no use. Seeing all the dead bodies lying around him, his mind seemed to snap. He wandered endlessly through the dark tunnels of the coal mine.

When he came to his senses, he realized that he was lost. He began running through the dark tunnels, looking for someone. Getting short of breath, he stopped to rest.

When he opened his eyes, he saw a white glow about twenty yards in front of him and, thinking it was the light from a miner's cap, ran toward it. When he reached the object, he stopped suddenly, as if he had seen a ghost. Lying against the ribbing was a human hand. From the gold braided ring on the third finger, he knew that the hand belonged to him. The index finger was pointing toward the south. It was strange, but Jim knew that he must follow the pointing finger.

When Jim found the crew working in Section Six Butt, he told them about the cave-in and about the hand, his hand, that had led him to safety. When they all laughed at him, he went back to the place where he had seen the hand glowing against the ribbing. He searched the whole section, but he couldn't find the hand. He knew now that nobody would believe his story, but he also knew that the pointing finger had saved his life.

69. *The Old Horse*

WHEN MY FATHER first started working in the Grant Town mine, the men had horses to pull the coal buggies instead of machinery as they have today. The horses were the men's best friends, and it was a sad day when they were taken out of the mines. One man liked the horses so much that he quit working when they were taken out. This story is about that man and how he became so attached to one particular steed.

My father started working the midnight shift when he first entered the mines, along with another buddy, Flora Santa. In those days a miner had to use a pick and shovel to dig out the coal, and it was hard work, especially if one ran into slate or sulfur balls. When the buggy was loaded, it would be pulled down to the mine shaft by a horse to unload the coal. The horses were often slow, and it usually took several hours to make the trip.

One night, when my father finished loading the buggy, Flora said he would take the load down to the tipple. It was supposed to be my father's turn to make the trip, but Flora said, "You're not as strong as I am, boy. You sit here and take it easy, and I'll make this trip for you."

My father was tired, so he didn't argue with Flora. To reach the tipple, Flora had to pass a section that had had a cave-in just a few days before. As Flora reached the section, the horse started whinnying. Flora cursed the horse under his breath for making so much noise. Then he heard a rumbling sound coming from overhead. Now he knew why the horse was making so much noise. The ceiling was caving in.

When Flora opened his eyes, he found that he was still alive. He was half covered with slate and he was almost choked from the rock dust that was in his mouth, but he was alive. With the help of his free hand, he was able to get out from under the slate pile. The horse too had lived through the cave-in. Dazed, Flora got to his feet and started walking in the direction of the tipple. He walked for a long time, but seemed to be getting nowhere. When he came back to the caved-in section, he knew that he had been walking around in circles. He sat down on a lump of slate and waited for someone to come and rescue him, but then he realized that nobody would come for him, because nobody knew that he was missing or hurt. My father wouldn't think anything had happened to him because he knew it usually took two or three hours to make the trip to the tipple. The men at the tipple would think that he and his buddy were still working up in their section. Flora was a goner and he knew it!

Flora felt the air getting heavy and knew that it was only a matter of time before all the oxygen would be used up. He laid his head against the side of the ribbing and prepared himself for death. Then he heard a deep, far-off voice say, "Get up, Flora. Get up, Flora."

Flora opened his eyes, but there was nobody in sight —nobody but the old horse. Thinking that he was only dreaming, he closed his eyes again. Just as he was about to give up, he felt something hot against his face, and the same voice said, "Get up, Flora. I'll show you how to get out of here."

When Flora shut his eyes again, the horse put his head against Flora's shoulder and turned him over on his side. Again the deep voice said, "Get up, Flora. Get up, Flora, and I'll lead you out of here."

More dazed than ever, Flora managed to get to his feet and follow the old horse. It was as if some spell were compelling him. When Flora came to his complete senses, he was at the tipple. He didn't tell anyone how he got out of the cave-in, because he knew no one would believe him.

Years later, when the horses were all replaced with machinery, Flora quit the coal mines. And he didn't quit because he was ready to retire. He quit because he knew that a piece of machinery could never take the place of an old horse.

70. Section South Main

"FIRE IN THE hole" is a familiar cry to anyone who has worked in the coal mines. It means that they are ready to blast for sulfur balls. Sulfur balls are the miners' most dreaded enemies. They are ten times harder than iron, and there isn't a drill that can drill through the hard ones. When somebody yells "Fire in the hole," it means that you must take quick action and cover yourself the best way you can.

Sometimes something goes wrong with the blasting. If the ribbing is weak, the whole ceiling will come down, covering up the section. That is exactly what happened when they blasted Section South Main in the Grant Town mine a few years ago. Six men lost their lives, but the strange thing was their bodies were never found. After that, the section was closed, but one still had to go through it on his way to other sections.

One night a buggyman* was on his way to pick up the men for the midnight shift. He had deposited one load and was on his way back with the empty mantrip to pick up another load of men. While passing through the dreaded section, he saw two swinging red lanterns on each side of the tracks. He stopped the buggy beside them and opened the mantrip doors for them to get in. When the buggy reached the miners, they waited for the buggyman to open the doors for them. When he did, the mantrip was empty, except for two burning red lanterns. They couldn't figure

* The "buggy" is a small locomotive used to haul cars in the mines; the "buggyman" is the driver. "Mantrip" is a car (sometimes a string of cars) used for transporting the miners.

it out, because they'd quit using red lanterns since the cave-in up in Section South Main.

A few weeks later two buddies, Hack Retton and Stanley Minlovitz, were working in the battery room. Since it was the midnight shift, they had nothing to do but wait until the batteries were charged. In the meantime, they could catch up on their sleep. When the batteries were charged, a bell would ring, telling them it was time to take off the charging units. All they had to worry about was getting caught by either the mine foreman or the section boss. Stan usually slept near the shack door so he could hear if anyone came near the battery shack.

It was about three o'clock in the morning when Stan was aroused from his deep sleep by footsteps outside. Thinking it was the foreman or section boss, he woke up Hack and they both went to the door. Six figures came walking toward them. They were six miners, swinging red lanterns, passing on their way toward Section South Main. As the last one passed the shack, he said in Polish, "Hi, Stan." Hack Retton didn't know the men, but Stan did. The one who spoke to him was an old buddy, who had been killed in the big explosion in Section South Main.

When the story got around to the other miners, they wouldn't go near the section and made another route around it. Today the section is sealed up with three yards of cement, but despite the thick walls, one can still hear cries coming from Section South Main.

71. The Blue Flame

ONE OF MY grandfather's friends was killed in a mine explosion. To make matters worse, the body could not be found by any of the men. The next day the dead man's son was forced to go to work in the same mine to make a living for the family. The boy was very frightened.

While working, the boy became separated from the others, around a twist in the mine. As he was trying to find his way out, he saw a blue flame. This blue light puzzled him, but he began to follow it. Sometimes he would lose sight of it, but it would always wait for him.

He followed it deeper and deeper into the mine. Every once in a while a rat would run by. Water dripped from the walls. The air got thinner. He became more frightened when he heard a voice call, "Davy! Davy!"

He followed the echoing voice on into the mine. All of a sudden he saw his father's image in the blue flame. He ran toward the flame and fell into a hole in front of his dead father. The missing body was found.

72. Big Max

BIG MAX is now a foreman for a large construction company in Cleveland, Ohio. He is a brown-skinned Negro, about six and a half feet tall and weighing about two hundred and fifty pounds. So it is easy to see how he got his name, and wherever he goes, it is not long before his name follows him.

When he worked in the mines, Big Max was known for his strength. He used to run from the Osage mine where he worked to his home, ten miles each way. One time a motorcar fell over on a man and pinned him from the waist down. Big Max lifted the car by himself and saved the man's life. He could load more coal than six ordinary men, and would stay in the mine for days—for as long as a week sometimes.

It seemed as though nothing could hurt him. One time there was a bad cave-in in the section where he was working. Everybody was killed but Big Max, and when the men found him, he had dug himself halfway out. Some of the miners looked on him as a kind of god of the mines. But Big Max left the coal mines. And this is the story he told my father:

After that bad explosion that closed off Section Five on the main run, all the men in the section were either killed or accounted for except one. He was never found. His timecard wasn't punched in or out. The mine officials would not pay his wife the welfare money because they thought he had deserted her. Well, anyway, I opened up the section and went in first to check and see if it was still "hot."* Our main job was to set in new beams and clean up the sections so new track could be laid. After I had checked the place completely for gas, I started helping the other men set beams.

In one of the subsections was a bad place, and since none of the other fellows wanted to chance putting in the new beams, I said I would go ahead and set in the first one for them. I went back into this dark section and was getting ready to put in the first beam, when one of the fellows came back to help. I said, "So you are not afraid after all?" and he said, "No."

It was then that I noticed that I had never seen him before. He did not look like a miner—at least, not like a healthy one. His skin, even though it was covered with coaldust, was milkish-white. His eyes were set deep in his head like deep wells. And although he could do as much work as me, he was just a bag of bones.

After we had put up the first beam, I started cleaning a place for the second beam. The man who was helping me grabbed the shovel and said, "Don't put that post there; put it here!" He said it real madlike, so to keep down an argument, I started doing as I was told.

I had cleaned about a foot of loose coal and slate when I hit something. It looked like a boot, like a man's boot.

* The word means here a dangerous content of combustible gases.

113

Just as I turned around to tell my helper that I had found the remains of a man, he disappeared. I didn't particularly think anything of it because I thought my eyes were playing tricks on me, since I hadn't been to bed in three days. And then, too, I thought he might have got scared and gone back. Well, anyway, I reported the body to the authorities and went home.

In the middle of the next night, I was sleeping soundly when there was a knock at the door. I went and opened it and discovered it was the fellow at the mine who had been helping me. He said, "Thank you for helping me. Now my wife will get what is coming to her." He disappeared again. I got dressed and went immediately to the mine to see just who this fellow was that I had discovered. He was the man who had been missing. They could tell by his miner's tags. I left the mine and have never, and shall never, set foot in a mine again.

73. *The Ghost of Jeremy Walker*

AFTER AN EXPLOSION at the Barrackville which killed a number of men, all of the bodies were found with the exception of an old colored fellow by the name of Jeremy Walker. The thing that the men who had worked with Jeremy remembered about him was his very boisterous laugh. He had worked on the cateye* shift and was always trying to help someone fill his quota of coal.

For the next eight years after Jeremy's death, until hand loading was no longer used in the mine, the men would always fill their quota of coal. Whenever one of the miners would go to the foreman and tell him that he had not filled his quota, the foreman would go back to check the

* This is the late shift, from 11 p.m. to 7 a.m.

amount loaded, and always find the quota filled. And a laugh like Jeremy's would be heard in the distance.

The reason for this mysterious happening was never discovered. But the men who work there now and the men who have since retired believe that the work was done by the ghost of Jeremy Walker.

74. *Post Inspection*

ON A COLD, wintry day in 1950, Mr. Barron reported for work as usual. Soon after he arrived at the Idamay mine, a horrible accident occurred.

Sam McCormick, a foreman, was coming out of the mine, riding on a motorcar. As he was rounding a curve, the car overturned, crushing Sam against the wall, killing him almost instantly. The cause of this fatal accident could not be determined. Perhaps it was excessive speed; no one knew.

After work in the mine had again returned to its regular pattern, Freedman, a colored fellow, was working in this same passage just on the other side of the airlock from where the accident had occurred. When he heard someone walking around outside, he assumed it was Mr. Barron, as he was due to come anytime. Freedman thought nothing of it and continued to work.

Some time passed by, and he could still hear someone walking around on the other side of the doors. Whoever it was would walk a while and then pause, walk some more and then pause again, just as though he were studying something. Freedman could stand this no longer, so he called, "Mr. Barron, is that you there?"

But there was no answer—just silence. Freedman started back to work, but just then he heard steps sounding once more. So he called again, "Mr. Barron, is that you?"

And still there was no answer. Not a word.

He became frightened and rushed to the doors, determined to find out who was there. Opening the doors and looking down the dusky passage, he could barely distinguish a figure bending over and apparently inspecting the rails. When he called, the figure straightened up and started walking toward him. When it came into the light, Freedman saw it was not Mr. Barron but Sam McCormick. He immediately slammed the doors shut and fell to the ground.

A short time later Mr. Barron did appear and found Freedman trembling violently. Upon hearing his story, Mr. Barron thought that Freedman must have fallen asleep, for he had just come straight down the passage and had seen no one.

75. *The First Husband of Mrs. James*

MRS. JAMES HAD been married before. Shortly after starting to work in the Grant Town mines, her first husband had burned to death in a fire, leaving her with two small boys to bring up. Times were hard then, and six months after her first husband's death, she had married Mr. James, who had been one of her husband's close friends.

Every morning after her second marriage Mrs. James would get up early, get her husband off to work, and then go back to bed. As soon as she would get in bed, her first husband would appear. Sometimes he would sit in a chair close to the bed; sometimes he would sit at the foot of it. He would just sit there and look at her for about five minutes and all at once he would disappear. For about a month he came like this, day after day.

Finally Mrs. James could stand it no longer and had to

be placed under a doctor's care. When she had recovered somewhat, her doctor advised her to go away from Grant Town for a while, so Mrs. James visited her mother and father in Jane Lew for a month. On her return to Grant Town she and her husband moved into a new house, almost half a mile from the old one.

For a while nothing unusual happened. But then one morning her dead husband reappeared and sat on the foot of the bed and stared at her. The next day he appeared again, and Mrs. James asked him, "In the name of God, what do you want?" He told her to come with him.

Mrs. James hurriedly dressed and followed her dead husband from the house. He led her toward the mine. When she arrived, she saw Mr. James about to enter the cage to go down into the mine. She called to him and he came running, thinking that something might be wrong. When he learned what had happened, he was angry, but he took Mrs. James into town to see a doctor instead of going to work.

On returning to Grant Town that afternoon, Mrs. James and her husband saw a crowd gathered around the mine. They went over to see what had happened and learned that there had been a slate fall where Mr. James would have been working and that ten men had been killed.

Mrs. James' first husband had saved Mr. James' life, and after that she and Mr. James put flowers on his grave every Memorial Day.

76. Possessed

FRED BROWN, a coal miner who is alive today and resides in Fairmont, lived with his brother John and John's wife in a part of town known locally as Rat Row. Fred worked at the old Gaston mine with Tony Jones, who also lives in Fairmont and is still alive.

117

One day in 1914 began a series of events which are remembered and talked about to this day. Fred, a normal, healthy man who was known and liked by everyone in the community, on this day changed suddenly and completely. It seemed as if he had become a different person. He stopped talking. He quit his job. He was unable to lift any significant weight, although he was known to be a man of great strength. He began to wear a tie, although he had never worn one previously.

His actions became so strange that people began to notice them more and more. Many reasons for his new behavior were advanced by the people of Rat Row, but none could satisfactorily explain it. Rose Cooper, a local resident, claimed he was possessed by the spirit of a dead person. With this idea in mind, she armed herself with a Bible and went to Fred's home to have a talk with him. When she arrived only Fred and John's wife were there.

Upon seeing Mrs. Cooper enter the door, Fred spoke up. "You finally came," he said.

Mrs. Cooper looked at him and asked, "How many of the spirits have returned with you?"

Fred refused to answer. Mrs. Cooper plied him with more questions, but still he remained silent. Finally she demanded, "In the name of the Father, of the Son, and of the Holy Ghost, talk."

At these words Fred at last broke his silence. When Mrs. Cooper asked him what he wanted, he replied, "I want my former landlady, Mrs. Thelma Parsons, to send money to a certain priest in Italy and have him say mass for me, with the tabernacle open."

This was an unusual request since the tabernacle remains closed during most of a mass in the Catholic Church.

"Who are you?" asked Mrs. Cooper, a chill creeping up her spine.

"I am Sam Vincci," he replied slowly.

At this, both women shivered with fright, for they knew who Sam Vincci was. He was a man who had been dead for two years—choked to death in a freak accident at the old Gaston mine.

Mrs. Cooper finally became calm enough to inquire of Fred—or was it Sam—"Why did you come back in Fred's body? We know that you were a decent man and cannot understand why you would do this to him."

The spirit answered by saying he wanted mass for himself and went on to thank Mrs. Cooper for treating him so kindly while he was alive.

Mrs. Cooper talked the spirit into letting her take care of the mass. She then asked it to leave Fred's body, but to do so in such a way that no one would be frightened.

The spirit agreed, and after causing Fred to rub his hands over his face, it appeared to leave Fred's body, for after that Fred seemed to return to normal. But later that night, after Mrs. Cooper had gone home, Fred walked into her home and, without a word, proceeded to sweep out the house. Had the spirit returned?

Mrs. Cooper wrote to the priest in Italy who said mass for Sam Vincci. Once more Fred returned to normal. The spirit had gone.

To this day Fred does not remember what happened during the three months the spirit possessed him.

13   Railroad Ghosts

Most of the railroad ghosts go back fifty or more years when new tracks were being laid and bridges and tunnels built and before modern safety devices and methods of operation were used. In those days accidents on the railroad were common and no doubt figured largely in the talk when railroadmen got together.

In West Virginia with its many hills the laying of track required numerous tunnels and cuts, and many men were killed in their excavation. These dark and lonesome spots with their memories of sudden death were especially suitable settings for mysterious happenings.

77. The Body under the Train

MY GREAT-GREAT-GRANDFATHER, Mr. Wilburn, was a track foreman on a section of the Baltimore and Ohio railroad from Terra Alta east. His house was two miles east of Terra Alta, on the opposite side of a deep cut. His house was large and his family small, so his wife boarded three of his laborers—Joe, a married man, and Bob and Dick, two bachelors.

Whenever they were paid, Bob and Dick usually spent the evening in Terra Alta. One payday it was Bob's misfortune to draw the job of inspecting the track. This would keep him from spending the evening in town. Because he needed the money, Joe volunteered to do the job. Bob and Dick went merrily on their way.

During the evening Dick was put in jail for drinking and disturbing the peace. Bob lost his payroll in a poker game. Mumbling to himself about his loss, he started down the track without a light.

Suddenly he realized he was approaching the cut. He recalled some of the stories of people who had gone through it alone. The cold wind whistled through the rails. It was so dark he could barely make out the outline of the top of the hill.

About midway through, he stepped on something—soft—not like a crosstie. It felt like an animal. Bending down to remove it from the track, he found a human head.

Bob was so frightened, it took my great-great-grandparents an hour to calm him. When they went to see what had happened, Mr. Wilburn and a neighbor found the head and body of Joe, who had been hit by a night passenger train.

Several days later, Bob quit his job. He said he kept seeing the headless form of a body under a coach of the night train. Mr. Wilburn tried to convince him there were no such things as ghosts, but Bob quit and left that part of the country.

78.   Boardtree Tunnel

DURING THE construction of the Boardtree Tunnel, there were a great many deaths due to accidents. A lot of men were killed by trains. Also, a cholera plague took the lives of many laborers and their families. A cemetery was made on top of the tunnel, and all the victims were buried there.

Billy Hogan was a section boss of one of the crews that worked on the tunnel. He was Irish and witty and a great character, according to report—always playing pranks on the men in his crew. But Billy was killed the day the tunnel was finished by the first train to go through it, and his body was buried in the cemetery on top of the hill.

After Billy's death, one of his good friends, an old Irishman named Packie Henderick, got the job of track-walker and also of taking care of the tunnel during the day. It was not long until Packie began telling tales of Billy being with him all day while he worked. He entertained all the country around with his tales.

He said he could always tell when Billy was in a bad mood. His fire would go out. His tools would be scattered about. Bricks would fall from the tunnel roof. Spikes would not go into the ties straight. Nothing would go quite right. When Billy was in a good humor, everything would go fine. He said that when he was walking the track, Billy would whisper to him and show him where there were faulty places in the ties or rails. He would share his lunch with Billy; other men going into the tunnel to work would occasionally find these bits of food that Packie had left for his friend Billy.

Some of the trainmen hated to go through the tunnel at

night. They claimed they would see a light at the opening that vanished when they approached. Whether this was Billy, no one ever knew for sure.

After Packie died, few people told the stories about Billy Hogan anymore.

79. The Headless Man

AROUND 1915 there used to be a long chain hanging down over the Baltimore and Ohio track at the depot in Fairmont to signal the engineer when to slow down. The chain would hit some part of the train and the noise would signal the engineer.

One evening about dusk one of the trainmen was on top of one of the cars. He wasn't paying any attention to what was ahead, and he didn't see the chain hanging over the track. The chain hit him just over the shoulders and wrapped around his neck. It snapped his head off, and he fell to the ground. The train went on because nobody at the time knew what had happened. Later when they learned about the accident, the railroad officials removed the chain.

People who would be walking the track about dusk where the chain had hung would see a lantern ahead. The closer they got to the lantern, the better they could see the figure of a man. And, sure enough, the man didn't have a head. As they got closer, they could see the headless man cross the track and then disappear.

Joe Board didn't believe in such things, so he decided to see for himself. But one night, as he walked down the track, he saw the lantern and then the headless man. Everyone thought this was the trainman looking for his missing head.

80. *The Phantom Wreck*

SHORTLY AFTER the turn of the century, in mid-April, an eastbound Baltimore and Ohio passenger train was descending into the valley near Rowlesburg during the early morning. Suddenly the train jumped the tracks and plunged down a 200-foot embankment. The sleeping passengers never knew what had happened. Seven were killed, many were injured, and a number of the injured passengers died later. Exactly what had caused this wreck no one could find out.

About seven years later two brothers were walking home from a card game and passed near the place of the accident. They both heard the whistle of a train. Knowing that none was due then and thinking it might be a wrecking train, they stopped to watch it come into sight. Instead, it was a passenger train. Before their eyes it jumped the tracks and crashed down the embankment at the Phil Hollow crossing. The boiler on the engine exploded and flames shot from the cars, but not a sound was heard. Just as the men were about to run for help, the wreck vanished, and when they went over to the embankment, there were no signs that anything had happened.

14   Animals and Birds

T HE BIRD and animal ghosts here are not human spirits who have returned in another form but are manifestations of actual creatures. There are possible exceptions; the mysterious sound of the nursing sow may be associated with the baby's death, and the appearance of the black cat, since nothing is known of its background in the story, may also have some human association.

A notable element in four of these stories is retribution. In three of the stories the creatures return to exact terrible payment for abuse they had suffered at the hands of men. In "The Phantom Dog" the animal, on the other hand, seeks revenge for its master's murder. Three of the remaining stories are less easy to define. The ghost of the canary apparently serves as a man's conscience, bringing about, not punishment, but a change of heart. The dismembered dog seems to display only the restlessness that frequently accompanies a violent, unreasonable death, and the nursing sow, which is only present audibly, may be explained in the same way, though the circumstances of its manifestation are not altogether clear. Only two of the eleven stories in this group represent an act of kindness on the part of the ghost.

As Louis C. Jones says in *Things That Go Bump in the Night* (p. 15), horses (no doubt including invisible horses, headless horsemen, phosphorescent horses, and other varieties) lead in the number of ghost animals, with dogs in second place. Ghost cats are not very common, although I have three other ghost cats. Usually they are more associated with witches than with ghosts. My cat seems merely to come back to carry on his usual way of life.

81.   *The Tortured Sparrow*

MORE THAN a hundred years ago, before the Civil War, and when this section was still a part of Virginia, there came to these parts a man from farther south in Virginia with his family—his wife, his son Caliph, and his mother-in-law. On the east side of the "River-of-Falling Banks," which was the Indian word *Monongahela,* was a village then known as Palatine, but now part of Fairmont.

South of Palatine, and up the Monongahela River a short distance, the man, whose name was Strode, purchased a steep and wooded tract of land. Across from what is now Fifth Street, on the flat below Palatine Knob, he built a log house. Nearby he built a smokehouse. In the smokehouse Strode had stored two barrels of salt, a valuable commodity in those times, and also had cured meat hanging.

Strode's mother-in-law was said to have become insane. But Strode was a man of evil repute and terrible temper, and there were many whispered stories that the old woman was not crazy at all. At any rate, Strode had her chained in the smokehouse. One cold winter, when the river was covered with ice and the snow was more than a foot deep on the mountain, the smokehouse caught fire and burned to ground. The people of Palatine, awakened by the red glow in the sky to the south, hurried toward it. When they arrived, the building was destroyed. Strode and some of his slaves had been able to roll out the two barrels of salt and carry out much of the meat, which was saved, but the mother-in-law was burned to death.

Strode's son Caliph was as mean a young man as ever lived in these parts. He was cruel to animals and was rude and overbearing. He was disliked heartily by all who knew him. He terrorized the slaves on his father's farm and abused and mistreated the animals.

One cold winter day Caliph Strode caught a live sparrow. He pulled all the feathers off the half-dead bird and then tossed it out into the snow. The bird managed to hop up on a low limb of a tree, where it sat, freezing and chirping. When morning came, the bird was still clinging to the limb of the tree, frozen stiff.

After that, Caliph Strode became meaner than ever. He also became nervous and sullen and appeared to be afraid. It was not long until he was a raving maniac. His mother, a poor downbeaten woman who seldom spoke, told some of the neighbor women that every night, when Caliph was sleeping, the frozen sparrow would come to the limb of a tree outside the window of his room and chirp, "Caliph, I'm cold! Caliph, I'm cold!"

It would continue calling until Caliph would awaken screaming. He moved his sleeping quarters to another room, but it did no good. He sat up all night before the open coal fire, but when he would doze in his chair, he would awaken screaming again. It was not long until his mind was gone. Until his death he was terrorized by the pitiful cries of the naked and freezing sparrow.

82. The Canary

EVERYBODY who works in the coal mines knows the importance of the canary. Miners love the canary, and always have—all but one man, Bill Toth. Bill didn't like any kind of bird. The only good bird to him was a dead one.

One day one of the canaries escaped from the cage and began flying around in the mines. Bill Toth was eating his lunch, when the canary flew down to eat some of the bread crumbs that were lying on the ground. Bill picked the bird up in his hands and crushed him. The bird was still kicking, so Bill picked it back up and tore one of its wings off. The other miners told Bill that he would get his punishment the same way someday. My father told Bill that the poor canary might have saved his life, but Bill just laughed.

Sometime later, Bill and another buddy were laying brattice cloth in preparation of digging into another section. When the brattice cloth was laid, the other man told Bill that he was going down the tracks to get a canary to find out if there were any signs of leaking gas in the new area. Bill told him not to go, but he went anyway. When the man left for the canary, Bill sat down to have a cigarette. It's against the law to smoke in the mine, but Bill told himself that there wasn't anybody around for miles.

Before Bill could strike his match, he heard a fluttering sound overhead. He turned around and a yellow canary landed on his shoulder. Bill picked up the bird and started to kill it, but he discovered that it was already dead! At first Bill thought the canary had died because of gas fumes in the section, but when he examined it, he found this was wrong. The bird had been crushed to death! When Bill examined the canary further, he found that one of its wings had been torn off. Then Bill remembered that he had done this same thing to a canary a few weeks before. Could this canary be the same one that he had crushed in his hands?

130

You may not think so, but, evidently, Bill did! Today he has two canaries in his house, and probably wouldn't part with them for the world!

83. *The Cat*

ONE TIME my father rented an old, hewed-log house with a double chimney; it had stood empty for several years. Since the house was very big and I was the only one of the children at home at the time, we decided to close off the upstairs part and just use the downstairs rooms. There was a door to the stairway on one side of the living room fireplace, so my father shut this door and locked it.

We were sitting in front of the fire one night, not long after we had moved in, when we heard a loud crash from the empty room above us. As we listened, the sound seemed to spread and turn into more of a rattling noise. It sounded exactly like somebody had dropped about a barrel of walnuts and the walnuts had spilled out all over the floor. We heard some of the walnuts—or whatever it was—hit the opposite wall, while some of them rolled down the stairs. They stopped rolling before they hit the stairway door— all of them but one, that is. It came on, bumpity, bump, bump . . . bump!

While we stared toward the door, a big, black cat came through the little, tiny crack at the bottom. It had flattened itself out some way, I suppose. We hardly had time to see it coming before it was there, on our side of the door.

It was the biggest, blackest, shiniest cat I ever saw. Without paying any attention to us, it walked over to the hearth and sat down. It looked into the fire, blinking its eyes, then started to lick itself. It worked at that for five or ten minutes, blinked at the fire some more; then, with us never taking our eyes off of it, it got up and walked back to the stairway and slid under the door.

Well, we didn't know what to make of this. We got a light and unlocked the door and looked all over the upstairs rooms. But we didn't find the cat, or any walnuts, or anything else.

Every week or so after that, we would hear the same noises and the cat would come again. Though it didn't seem to wish us any harm, my father soon got tired of the racket that went with it. One night when the "walnuts" had poured out and it was sitting on the hearth washing itself, the way it always did, Pa said, "Henry, let's kill that daggone cat."

For the first time, the cat looked at us. It bowed itself up, its eyes glared like fire, and sparks flew from its fur. I grabbed the broom anyway, and swarped it down over the cat. But the cat wasn't there. We saw it run into the kitchen. My mother got the lamp, and we took after it. I had two or three chances to kill it but, for some reason, I couldn't hit it at all. Finally, after I had knocked down everything else in the house, my father called from the front room that the cat had gone back under the door.

We hoped we had scared it into staying away, but after the usual time, it was back sitting by the fire, just as if nothing had happened.

My father said that since we couldn't get rid of it, we might as well get used to it. So that's what we did, during the year that we lived there.

84. The Bench-Legged Dog

BEFORE THE Civil War, I lived in a little house on the run back of Barrackville. Once as I was passing not far from a house, I saw a heavy-bodied, bench-legged dog standing on a big, flat stone by the side of the path. It had its bristles all up, was showing its teeth, and acted like it was going to attack me at once. It was five or six steps away, and I had nothing to fight it with. I stomped my foot and said, "Git out!" but it paid no attention.

I saw a stone nearby, bent down and picked it up to throw at the dog, but when I straightened up to throw, the dog was gone. I looked all around but saw no dog. There was not a thing near that the dog could have got behind to hide. There was not a thing for some distance around that could cover him, but he was gone. I dropped the stone that I had picked up and went on home.

When I got home, a neighbor's wife was there talking to my wife. I at once began to tell about the dog I had seen; the neighbor woman roared out laughing and said, "You have seen Mr. Straight's dog."

"What do you mean by Mr. Straight's dog?"

Then she said, "Did you never hear tell of Mr. Straight's dog?"

I said, "No."

Then she said, "Well, several years ago, a family by the name of Straight lived in the house you were passing. They had a child about three years old that played around the yard and out in the road. A bench-legged dog attacked the child, and it was badly bitten. The mother ran up, kicked the dog, picked the screaming child up, and started to the house.

"Just then two neighbor men came along. They were both staggering drunk. They caught the dog, and while one of them held its hind legs off the ground, the other one beat it to death with a club. Then they took the dog to that flat rock, all the time swearing and cursing and damning the dog to Hades and every other place they could think of. They got out their knives, cut the dog's throat from ear to ear, stuck their knives in its body, cut it open, took its heart out, cut it in slices, then cut it up into little pieces, swearing like troopers all the time.

"They left the remains on the rock, and someone took

them away the next day. A short time after that, a neighbor was passing one evening and saw the dog standing on that flat rock. He looked for something to hit it with, but when he looked back, it was gone. Since then more than a dozen people have seen that dog, always in the same place and about the same time in the evening. It always disappears in the same way."

85. The White Wolf

ABOUT A HUNDRED years ago in a little community called French Creek, in the Backbone Mountain region, lived a tall, slim man by the name of Bill Williams. He was better known as Hank the Shank or just plain Butch, because by trade he had been a butcher. When the state put a bounty on timber wolves, he gave up butchering cattle and turned his attention to killing wolves.

After he began to hunt, he bought himself a small cabin about five miles beyond the community. He kept a cow and a couple of pigs, which he let run loose in the forest.

Before he started hunting, he had spent all his time in the community general store. But after becoming a hunter, for several years he was rarely seen by the people of the community. He would come in for supplies about once a month and always at about nine o'clock at night.

For five years he hunted wolves and averaged more than five hundred a year. For each pelt, he got a bounty of ten dollars. When you add this up, it is better than five thousand dollars a year, and back in those days this was very good pay.

After five years, he had thinned out the wolves so much that they had almost become extinct, and the few that were left had become so smart and wary that they were never seen. So, again Bill started to spend a great deal of his time in the general store. He would come into the store when it opened in the morning and stay until it closed in the evening. He would just sit around, chew tobacco, whittle on a piece of wood, and talk about the weather and how things used to be, but most of all about his hunting expeditions.

Everything went well for a few years. Then one afternoon a man burst into the store, telling of a white wolf killing two of his sheep. He claimed that he had shot the wolf three times, but the bullets didn't seem to harm it. Several times that week there were animals killed, and several times the wolf was shot, but bullets seemed to have no effect upon it.

When the people found they couldn't hurt the wolf or stop it from killing their stock, they called on Bill to see what he could do about it. But he refused to hunt the animal, because, he said, the wolves had made him rich, and he had sworn never to harm another one.

The white wolf went on killing, unmolested, for two weeks, and then one night it killed Bill's pet cow. This was a fatal mistake for the wolf because Bill was so angry that he forgot all about the promise never to harm another wolf and swore to get revenge.

The next morning he went to town, bought a young lamb, and headed for the hills. He went back into the hills a good way and tied the lamb to a tree for bait. Then he backed off about fifty yards and sat down under another tree.

A few days later, when Bill failed to return, the townspeople set out to search for him. They found him still sitting against the tree, and the lamb still tied to the other tree, unharmed. Bill was dead, with teeth marks in his throat. The soft loam around him didn't have a track in it besides Bill's own, and there was no sign of a struggle.

After that, the white ghost was never seen again. Some say that when the moon is full, they can hear him baying.

86. The Phantom Dog

WHEN I WAS still in the pinfeather stage of boyhood, there was a story told in the village of Roanoke of a man who rode into the village one day on a beautiful sorrel horse, followed by a shepherd driving dog. He was a cattle buyer looking for cattle, and on the next day went back into the hills to bargain with a family for some cattle. He was never seen or heard of again.

A while later some of the village people who had grown suspicious at the man's disappearance came upon the dog near the top of a high point overlooking the village. The dog had worn a path completely around the hill except at one place where he would jump up on a six-foot thick chestnut log and then jump down again. Many who came to see the "dog ring," as it was called in the neighborhood, thought that perhaps the dog's master had been sitting there when he was killed.

Someone finally shot the faithful dog and, tying a heavy stone to the body, threw it into the river. But after nine days the body was seen floating just beneath the surface.

This unusual happening doubled the suspicions of the village. The suspected family were kept under close watch. Men hid in and about the fields where they worked or followed them about at night, hoping to overhear some word that would solve the mystery, but the word was never spoken.

Then one day a beautiful young woman rode into Roanoke on a sorrel horse, a dead match for the one ridden by the man who had disappeared. The woman was seeking for news of her husband. When she heard about the man, the horse, and the dog, she was sure that this had been her husband, and she turned around and went sadly to her home near Johnstown.

The people of the vicinity were more suspicious than

ever and continued spying on the suspected family, but still they could discover nothing.

Soon, though, this family seemed to have acquired some wealth. They bought more land, more cattle, and more of everything. The village people would have nothing to do with the family.

Finally one of the men began to break under the strain. He drank heavily, and when he was drunk, he would see the shepherd driving dog. He would throw stones at it and would curse and cry, but the dog remained to plague him. Strange to say, no one else was ever able to see the dog. The man sold out and moved to a distant part of the region, but the dog followed. Finally he sold all his holdings and moved to the Far West. Whether the dog followed him there we never knew.

87. The Old Sow

THE FIRST PERSON who encountered the hog was a young, active man by the name of Hudon Thompson. One dark night he was following the road home over the hill near our house. At a certain place he heard a peculiar noise but could not locate it. Being a man of good courage, he walked on unconcerned. The sound followed him. He pulled his gun and shot several times, but the sound continued. Then he started running for home. The sound followed to the top of the hill and there died out suddenly.

In telling the story to my father and others, he remarked, "It just sounded like a big, old sow, grunting to her suckling pigs—except it was so pitiful."

My father laughed and said, "You just heard a real hog, and it sounded different on account of the darkness of night and the lonely road."

"I was not scared," Thompson said, "and I do not spook

easily. That thing followed me—and kept up, which convinces me that it was no hog. I never saw a hog that could have paced me, going up that road."

Soon afterward the Fisher boys were in that section, hunting at night. Their dogs came in, scared and bristling —followed by the jerky grunting of a sow, giving suck to her pigs. The Fisher boys did not remain to count the litter, but set out for home at a gait that left the dogs falling behind. Their story was laughed off, as had been Thompson's.

Then a farmer by the name of Hull heard the noise one night, at just about the same spot that Thompson had heard it. He, too, gave it territory undisputed. Again the skeptics laughed, my father the loudest of all.

One midday my older brothers and sisters went to get some apples from the farm that was the lair of the phantom hog. They were busy gathering apples about noon, when Watch, the big, black hound that was their constant companion, began to growl, show his teeth, and lift his hackles. The children took refuge in the apple tree. Then, they heard it—the pitiful grunting of a hog. It seemed to come from all sides, and the dog, trying to guard the children, ran this way and that, and jumped and growled like it had lost its senses. The children left their perches in the apple tree and made a run for home, with the hog everywhere and the dog at their heels. I was but a small child, but I clearly remember seeing them come down the hill and remember the excited chatter with which they told their story.

Again my father laughed and chided them for running from an imaginary hog. "I never thought I would father children who lacked courage," he remarked.

"We weren't scared," one of the older boys said. "Dad, there is something back there. It even scared old Watch. I don't know what the damned thing is, but it sounds mighty like a sow pig."

Then on a warm, rainy night that autumn, Newt

Hawkins, W. A. West, and my father took the lantern, called the dogs, and climbed the hill toward the chestnut flats to catch some coons. They topped the rise that led to the flats and chestnut groves. Soon the dogs were baying on a coon trail, and the hunters leaned back against a large chestnut tree to listen to the chase and mark the progress of the dogs. There was a soft drizzle of mist falling, and the night was pitch-dark. In an interval between the baying of the dogs there came to the ears of the three hunters the grunting of a sow nursing her pigs.

"Will, what in the devil's name is that?" my father asked.

"It's that damned hog that has been chasing people for years," Hawkins stated. "Let's find it if it takes all night."

The three men began the search. They separated, and wherever each went, there was the noise all about. They converged and separated time and again with the same result. Then they came together and sat down near the tree where they had first heard the sound. It was there about them, grunting, "Eh—eh—eh," over and over. They gave up and came home, the phantom hog following them to the line fence that marked our farm.

The only explanation that anyone could think of was an incident that had occurred years before. Some hunters had seen their dogs drag something from a hollow chestnut log. Upon investigating, they had discovered the charred remains of a newborn baby, which people supposed had been put there by a member of a family who lived on that branch and had had no good reputation among their neighbors.

88. The Junkman's Horse

THERE WAS a junkman living in the town of Plainview (now Monongah) about 1830 who was notorious for abusing his horse. The horse had taken its daily whipping and cursing for about fifteen years, but one day, it could take no more. It just lay down and died.

This only made the junkman angrier. He kicked and beat the dead horse until the townspeople came and dragged him off to stay in the town jail until he calmed down.

After that, people could hear the old horse pulling the junk wagon down the street every moonless night. On several occasions the horse was seen walking down the street where the junkman lived.

Then, one dark night, the town was awakened by the trampling of horse hoofs and the screams of a man. When people got to where the sound had come from, they found the junkman dead in a sandpile. He had been killed by a horse, but no tracks were found in the soft sand around the body. Only on the body itself did the hoofprints show.

The junkman's horse was never seen or heard again. There was no doubt in the people's minds as to what had happened. The horse had gotten its revenge.

89. Jack

ERIC WAS GETTING old, and the horse, Jack, that was assigned to him would soon be beyond working, as far as the mines were concerned. Eric had the job of taking coal cars back and forth in the mines, and for four years he had been working the job with Jack. The two of them got along well, and Eric took extra good care of Jack. Many of the men in the mines said jokingly that Eric thought more of Jack than he did of his wife. In the time they had been together, they had become more or less a legend in the mines, for Eric and Jack could haul more coal than any of the other haulers.

Eric made good money, for he was paid by the number

of cars he hauled. He repaid Jack by bringing extra grain into the mines, and every night before he left the stable, he would rub Jack down and put fresh hay out for the horse.

The day came when Jack was no longer able to haul the heavy coal cars, so he was taken out and replaced. Eric did not fail his faithful horse. He bought him from the company. He planned to use Jack for odd jobs in the summer, like plowing gardens and hauling wood and rock.

Time passed quietly, with Eric working his new horse in the mines every day, but he never failed to stop in the evenings to see Jack and rub him down.

One day in early spring Eric was hauling empty cars into a section of the mines where coal was to be loaded later in the day. He came to the trapdoor which separated the section from the main tunnel. As he approached the door, he was surprised to see Jack barring his way. Eric was frightened and went to get the boss, who laughed at the story. But Eric refused to take the cars in, and none of the miners would enter; and no amount of threats could persuade the men to do so.

The fire boss decided to show them how silly they were, so he went in himself. This all happened during the days when most of the men wore carbide lamps which had open flames. The fire boss, though, had an electric lamp. He also carried a canary to check for gas. When he entered the section, the canary in the cage dropped over dead, and the boss almost passed out, for the section was full of gas.

If Eric had entered with his carbide lamp, the section would have exploded, killing him and an unknown number of other men.

The men all felt that Jack was responsible for saving their lives, and when quitting time came, they went with Eric to see the horse. When they arrived at Eric's house, his wife told him that Jack had died that morning, at about the time Eric had seen him in the mines.

They buried Jack with much sorrow, and all the families attended. They felt that because of the kind treatment Eric had given the faithful animal, the horse, by some miracle, was able to repay his master by saving his life.

90. The Strange Chicken

ONE NIGHT MY grandfather and his family were riding home in their buggy. As they were passing the graveyard, they saw a chicken in the road, and it would not move out of their way. No matter what direction Grandfather moved, the chicken moved also, making it impossible for him to pass. Grandfather's daughter was with him, and she wanted to take the chicken home to feed it and let it get warm.

They took the chicken with them and, after arriving home, they put it on the mantel in the same room with the new baby so that it could get warm. Grandfather, Grandmother, and their daughter went into the kitchen to get something to eat. While they were eating, they heard a strange voice from the living room saying, "I want something to eat."

They knew it couldn't be the baby because it was too young to talk. They went into the living room, and there they saw the chicken sleeping contentedly. Then suddenly the chicken said, "I want something to eat!"

This frightened my grandparents, and Grandfather promptly grabbed the chicken and cut off its head.

The next day as Grandfather passed the grave of one of his relatives, he saw on the gravestone a large spot of blood. As he came closer to the grave, he could see that the blood was fresh. Grandfather was sure that the chicken had been his relative in disguise. He reasoned that when he had cut the chicken's head from its body, he had caused the spot of blood to appear on the grave marker.

91. A Loyal Dog

MANY YEARS AGO a small boy saw a little dog floating down the river on a log. He swam out, rescued the dog, and took it home with him. After this, the boy and the dog were together at all times. The dog lived for almost twenty years, and when it died, the young man was very sad to see his good friend go.

Sometime later the young man was walking through a field, when all at once he was pulled down by something behind him. This gave him quite a start, but when he looked around, he saw, just in front of him, a great crack in the ground. Had he not been stopped, he would probably have fallen into it and been killed.

What saved him, he did not know. There was nothing around that could have knocked him down or that he could have stumbled over. When he examined his clothing, however, there were the marks of a dog's teeth on his coat, and clinging to the coat some dog hair—the same color as his old dog's.

15   Weird Creatures

THE CREATURES in these stories are difficult to identify or explain. Unlike ordinary ghosts, which have some kind of rationale, creatures seem to have no connection with the real world. They sometimes resemble real animals, but are never quite like them, and frequently they are seen as fearful and destructive, though the human beings that they attack always manage to escape somehow. Nothing apparently affects them, not even silver bullets. The very mystery about these creatures may be the reason for their appeal.

"Old Wall-Eyes," in Vance Randolph's *The Devil's Pretty Daughter*, represents a slightly different type of creature story. Here the story appears to have been made up to entertain children. Like other ghost tales, the creature stories presented here are held by their narrators to be accounts of actual events.

92. *The White Thing*

THE NIGHT WAS damp and chill, and the forest stood dark and ominous as four elderly fox hunters sat hovering over a glowing mass of red embers. As if affected by their surroundings, the conversation drifted to supernatural legends. Many tales were told, but most of them centered on the White Thing, which supposedly inhabited the very region where they were now resting.

One of the men related an actual experience as told by his grandmother, who had lived nearby. She had taken her favorite mare to church one Saturday night, years ago. As she was riding back, within two miles of her home, she heard an unearthly scream. The mare bolted and thrashed her hoofs into the air. That was when she saw the White Thing, a raging bundle of white, bursting out of the woods beside her. It appeared to be much larger than a dog, yet not nearly a horse's size. Bearing a coat of pure white fur and razor-sharp teeth that jutted outward from a gigantic mouth, it moved on all fours and screamed like a woman in terrible agony.

Desperately the girl spurred her mare on, and finally the monster drifted back into the darkness behind her. At length she came to her land and an outlying barn. In her haste to reach the house which was still a good distance away, she left the mare untied and the barn door ajar. Seconds later, with a sigh of thankfulness, she entered the sanctuary of her home.

The following morning, she and her father planned to search for the animal's tracks. But at the barn they found her mare crumpled awkwardly against the door. Most of

the flesh was torn from its bones, and a look of stark terror was on its face.

93. *The Strange Creature*

IT WAS NIGHT, and the rain was coming down as if the sky were trying to dry itself of all the moisture it had. The lightning flashed for what seemed to be minutes at a time. The wind tried to pull the leaves from the trees and blow the windows from the house.

Inside, the men were getting ready to go to bed, until the night was pierced by a shrill scream that all but paralyzed everyone in the house. Uncle Will jumped up and grabbed his gun, as did his son and son-in-law. All three ran out into the storm. After the men left, the women bolted the doors.

Uncle Will met his older son coming from his house down the lane. As the four hurried toward where the scream had come from, a figure loomed ahead. All four shot, and again the scream was heard. Then all was quiet. The men advanced cautiously to the place where the figure was last seen, but in the dark they could find nothing.

Morning came at last. The rain had stopped, and the men went out into the field very early. The sight that met their eyes was not pleasant. They found four sheep badly mauled, with their throats cut, but no blood anywhere.

Several weeks passed, and little was said about what had happened to the sheep. Then one evening it started to rain again, and this time the men were ready. They bundled up, and again the strange cry was heard. They went deep into the field, and again they saw the bulky figure. Unable to tell whether it were standing on four feet or two, they took careful aim at the creature, which did not seem to notice that anyone was near.

Again four shots were fired. A scream, unearthly and

spine-tingling, rent the air. The men lit lanterns and ran through the muddy field. When they got to the spot, however, nothing was there but the remains of a sheep with its back broken and its throat cut. They buried the sheep and went back to the house.

To this day they do not know what it was they shot at, but they were never bothered by it again.

94. Shortcut

ON A HOT night in July, 1929, my father had started home at about twelve o'clock after finishing work at the 93 mine in Fairmont. He was extremely tired that night because he had worked an eleven-hour shift. Suddenly, as he started up a path, he saw something in front of him. It was white and stood about two feet from the ground. It had an extremely big head for its body and a fat, bushy tail. It jumped on my father several times.

My father had his lunch pail in his hands and started swinging it and kicking with his feet at the creature, but he said it was just like hitting at the air. The whole thing was strange, because the creature made no noise and its body seemed to have no substance.

Still the thing kept jumping up at him, and my father kept trying to fight it, but near a cemetery the creature just disappeared.

When my father reached the house, he looked at his arms and legs, but there was no sign of a scratch on them or on his body. He said he shook that whole night and just couldn't sleep, although he was very tired.

After that night, he refused to go home that way again. He went another way that took twice as much time. But, even today, what it was that attacked him that night still remains a mystery to him.

95. The White Figure

To GET TO their home from church, a couple had to pass a cemetery. One beautiful winter night they had been to church and were on their way home, when they had a strange experience. As they approached the cemetery in their horse and buggy, a white figure appeared. It resembled a dog, but was somewhat larger.

The horses reared up, and the young couple were thoroughly frightened, but they finally got the horses under control and got away. They thought it might have been only their imagination, so they did not mention the episode to anyone.

A few weeks later the same thing occurred when they passed the cemetery, and then they heard of similar experiences from other people. The wife became so afraid that she would hide in the buggy as they passed the cemetery, but still the figure appeared.

These experiences went on for several years, and then the wife died and was buried in the cemetery. Since that time, the white figure has never been seen by anyone.

The belief of some people is that the white figure wanted this woman, and it appeared at the cemetery, looking for her. Then when she died, it did not bother anyone else.

16   Immigrant Ghosts

WEST VIRGINIA, with the many diverse nationalities brought in by mining, is rich in the number of European ghost tales which may be found there. The five tales included here are a selection from a much larger number I have collected and are presented as typical examples. One feature that will be noted immediately is that all of these tales derive from central and southern Europe, areas which have contributed the greater proportion of the European population of the state.

One of the interesting things about these European tales are the national beliefs that are shown in them. For example, the Italian stories favor the theme of the possession of a living body by the spirit of a dead person; I have some half a dozen Italian variations of this theme. In the Balkans it is the vampire theme which is most common.

Yet another notable feature of the European ghost tales I have found in West Virginia is the malevolence of the spirits in them. Few of these wandering souls are kind or helpful. Perhaps the European tales, rooted in an older tradition, retain more of the fears of early man.

96. Seven Bones

A LONG TIME ago in Czechoslovakia, a young girl, whose mother was dead and whose lover had gone to war, went to an elderly fortuneteller to find out whether her lover was dead or alive. The old lady told her to get seven bones from seven different graves and boil them in a pot of water until midnight for seven nights. She said that at midnight on the seventh night her lover would come to her. If he were alive, he would be on foot, but if he were dead, he would be riding a horse. If he were a good spirit, the horse would be black, but if he were an evil spirit, the horse would be white.

About this time there was an epidemic in the country. So many people had to be buried that all old, unidentified graves were opened and the bones thrown out to make room for the newly dead. The girl did as she was told. She took seven bones from seven different graves and put them in a pot to boil each night. As the bones boiled, they said, "Putce, putce, putce," meaning, "Come, come, come."

On the seventh night the bones boiled harder and harder, and as the time neared midnight, they said louder and louder, "Putce, putce, putce," and suddenly the girl heard someone coming. She knew that it was her lover and that he was riding a horse. As she looked in the direction from which he was coming, she saw that the horse was white.

The old woman had told her to prepare seven bundles of cloth to take along and to take her rosary with her if she left home—so she did. When her lover asked her to get on the horse behind him, so they could ride away to be married, she did as she was told. As they galloped along, he said,

> "How the moon brightly shines,
> How the horse swiftly runs!"

And as they went farther and farther from home, he repeated the words, somewhat changed,

> "How the moon brightly shines,
> How the ghosts swiftly glide!"

Finally they came to a church and a cemetery, and the girl realized this was probably her lover's burial place. When he asked her to get down, she suggested that he get down first so that he could help her, which he did. But she threw the seven bundles in different directions, and the spirit-lover tore each of them apart before he tried to pursue her. The girl got down on the opposite side of the horse, ran to a nearby cottage as fast as she could, went in, bolted the door, and hung her rosary over the door knob.

In one corner of the cottage were some chickens, and on a bench, stretched out, was a dead man. The lover had reached the door by this time, and when he found it was bolted, he asked the dead man to unbolt it for him. The dead man replied that he, too, was an evil spirit and could not open the door because a rosary hung over the knob. The ghost-lover then went to one side of the cabin and started to try to scratch out the sides with his clawlike hands.

The girl turned to the chickens and begged the rooster to crow, so that the spirits would have to vanish, but the rooster said, "No, I won't crow for you. When you fed the chickens, you always chased the rooster away, so why should I help *you*?"

In the meantime the ghost-lover had called upon the dead man to help him claw out the side of the cabin, and he did. Again, the girl turned to the chickens and begged the rooster to crow, promising him, if he would, she would never again chase the rooster away when she fed the chickens.

So the rooster crowed, the ghost-lover vanished outside, the dead man lay back on his bench, and the girl was saved.

97. The Corpse That Wouldn't Stay Buried

IT WAS THE custom in Czechoslovakia for young men to go into the army at the age of twenty-one and serve for six years. A young man named Philip had served but three years when he was killed. His body was returned home and properly buried in the cemetery.

The next day the caretaker found the grave open and the open coffin beside it, as if it had never been buried. This was very strange, and many people wondered about it. The priest and the caretaker reburied the soldier, but the next day the same thing happened. After the third time, the caretaker put the coffin in the cottage where he kept his tools and equipment.

Time went on, and people no longer talked of the soldier who would not stay buried. The caretaker had a hen, and she went every day to the cottage, flew up to the coffin, and laid an egg beside the feet of the soldier. When the caretaker wanted to take the eggs, a voice spoke up, "Leave them alone. They are not to be taken yet."

This frightened him, and he left them alone. He even made jokes about this soldier who would not remain buried and yet kept eggs for himself, even though he could not eat them.

There lived in the village a very pretty and popular girl. Young Philip and she had been very much in love. After he had gone into the army, she was courted by many suitors. She was very sad when she learned of his death, but in time let herself be persuaded by her mother and father to marry someone else. As was the custom, everyone in the village was invited to the wedding feast to partake of the music, dancing, drink, and food. At such times there was always much gaiety and also much foolishness— but all in good fun, for everyone was happy at a wedding.

When the bride and groom returned from church, many of the older guests were already warm with wine. Almost everyone was full of jests, and one man got up and challenged anyone to go to the caretaker's cottage and get the eggs from the dead soldier. One man, who had had more wine than the others and was already unsteady on his feet, accepted the challenge. All the guests clapped their hands and urged him on. A wager of drinks was set up, and he left.

At the caretaker's cottage he started to put the eggs into his hat when a voice spoke up, as if from the soldier, although he did not see the lips move. "Since you take the eggs to the wedding, you will have to take me too."

Thinking this a jest, the man answered boldly, "Why not? There is always room for more at a feast. Put your arms around my neck and I'll carry you." And he did.

When the drunken guest reached the bride's home, he left the soldier outside, propped up against the wall by the door, where he stood, stiff and tall, his eyes closed as if he were a sentry asleep at his post. Only one arm moved out a little.

The drunken guest took the hat full of eggs to his fellow conspirators, won the bet of extra drinks and applause, and was quite content. But the soldier at the door put a hush on the festivity, and some of the guests did not speak kindly of the man who had brought him there. He told them that the soldier had asked him to bring him, so he could do nothing else.

Everyone knew that there must be some reason that the soldier would not remain buried—that his soul was not at peace—and speculated about what unfinished deed was troubling him so that he could not rest.

Finally the priest, who was also at the wedding, asked that everyone pray for the release of the poor soldier's soul so that he could go back to the grave where he belonged. But after the amen, the soldier still stood there, stiff and straight, and would swing out his arm as if wanting to shake hands. The priest said perhaps the soldier wanted to bid farewell to all his good neighbors and friends, so everyone lined up and went by and shook hands with the soldier.

The bride was last. She was very pale. She knew why he was there, but still had not said anything. When she put her hand into the soldier's, he clasped it tight and would not let it go.

Finally, with great weeping, she confessed that she and Philip had made a vow to marry only each other, and she had broken the vow by marrying someone else. Still the soldier would not let go of her hand.

The priest thought a moment and said, "Very well, you made your vow. You can still keep it. I shall say the marriage vows over you here and now."

And thus it was. When the final amen was said, the soldier let go of the bride's hand and vanished—in the twinkling of an eye—as if he had never been there. When the guests went to the caretaker's cottage, they found that the coffin and body were gone. The open grave was filled up and even a fine sod covered it. The soldier's soul was at rest.

98. Draga's Return

THERE IS AN old saying in Yugoslavia that if a cat crosses the body of a dead person, the spirit of that person will reappear as a ghost. Such a fantastic thing happened to the body of Draga Vellich. The family had been careful that a cat did not come near the body, but a window was left open near the coffin. A hungry cat jumped to the window sill and then across the body.

The first night after Draga was buried, his spirit returned to haunt his family. His wife was awakened by his cold arms about her and his cold lips kissing her. A strange noise was heard by all—a roaring, rolling noise—so penetrating that the whole house seemed to shake. Draga's wife and the surrounding neighbors were terribly frightened. But it all stopped in the early morning when the cock began to crow.

After repeated visits of the ghost, Draga's wife went to the priest and told him of the strange happenings. He told her, when the ghost returned, to tie some thread from a spool to the spirit as it caressed her, and in the morning they would follow the thread to see where it might lead.

The following night the ghost returned, and Draga's wife followed exactly the instructions of the priest. The next morning the priest and some men followed the thread to the grave of Draga. The priest told the men to get a long, sharp stake. They ran the stake through the grave, the coffin, and the body of Draga. This stake held the spirit down in the grave, and no longer was Draga's wife haunted by it.

99. The Old Crossroads

THE DELUCO FAMILY lived near the old crossroads on the outskirts of St. Giovanni, Italy. Mr. Deluco's family consisted of his wife and fifteen-year-old daughter Theresa. His sister lived on a neighboring hill with her two sons. Two nights before, these sons had been murdered at the crossroads, and the police could find no clues to the murderer.

A few days afterward, Theresa was going past the crossroads into the village, singing as she walked. She was startled by two large flies which flew down her throat. They seemed to have some strange control over her tongue. She was forced to say things of which she knew nothing. She ran home to her parents, all the while saying mysterious things. By the time she reached home, her arms and legs were badly swollen.

Her parents started to take her to the doctor, but when they reached the crossroads, she gagged and choked, and a voice said from her mouth, "Do not cross the crossroads, but go back the other way and find our killer, or we will cause the girl to choke."

The parents, horrified at these words, stopped immediately. Then, thinking the girl was hysterical, they tried to cross the road, but were stopped short by the girl's gasps and screams of agony. Terrified, they rushed her back home. They put her to bed, still swollen and still saying weird things. Because her swelling increased, they decided to try to take her to the village doctor again the next day.

She was calm and quiet until they reached the crossroads. Then she began to shake and uttered these words: "Nothing is wrong with Theresa, but turn back on the other road and you will find our murderer. Go the other way, or she will choke. Do not take her to the doctor, for there is nothing wrong. Go! Go!"

The many villagers who had gathered to see the girl

attempt to cross the road were astonished by her strange words. After seeing and hearing her speak, they were ready to satisfy her mysterious wishes. All together they went down the road which led to a number of houses. The girl's uncontrolled voice directed them to a small house beyond the others. The voice commanded them to stop and enter the house, where they would find enough evidence to solve the mystery.

But before they could enter the house, a half-crazed giant of a man rushed out and attacked the crowd with a blood-stained hatchet. But the men easily seized him and held him fast. Immediately, the swelling in the girl's arms and legs began to leave, and she spoke as herself again. She opened her mouth wide, and two flies flew out and away. Thus everyone knew that they had been led to the murderer by the spirits of the two slain brothers.

100. Footprints in the Snow

IN THE QUIET little village of Lutza in western Hungary lived Stefan Lutza, whose grandparents had founded the village over a hundred years before. Stefan followed the family tradition by becoming the mayor of the village that bore his name. It was the custom for the mayor to live in the big house that overlooked the village and to give shelter to all travelers that entered Lutza. But six years had passed, and no one had come to visit the mayor and his pretty young wife Esther.

Then one winter there came a knock on the door at midnight.

The snow was still falling as Esther got out of her warm bed. "I'll answer the door," she told her husband. "You go and see if the guest room is in order."

Stefan knew that he should be the one to answer the door and Esther to attend to the guest room, but he knew that she always was delighted when she met people for the first time. So, without offering a word of protest, he wrapped a heavy robe around his body and headed for the guest room.

"I'll make him stay until the snow melts," Esther said to herself.

She didn't know why she knew the knocker was a man. She gave her hair an extra pat and then opened the door. Through the snow a tall, dark stranger emerged into the light of the room. The two figures stood silently for some time, and then, as if the whole thing had been agreed upon, Esther and the dark stranger departed into the falling snow.

Alarmed that she had not appeared with the guest, Stefan called out for his wife. Getting no reply, he dropped his robe on the floor and hurried down the single flight of stairs. The door was wide open and white snowflakes fell lazily on the floor. From the lamp he was holding he could see tiny footsteps leading down the winding path. Stefan followed them, walking for nearly an hour before he realized that he, too, was barefooted.

He swung the lantern around and discovered he was in the village graveyard. Frightened, he ran more feverishly than ever along the single track of footprints, until they entered one of the tombs. Even before Stefan opened the wooden casket, he knew that the tomb belonged to his family. The casket lettering read, "Piztau Lutza, 1782-1852, settled and founded the village of Lutza in 1799." It was empty, except for shredded black rags that had once served as the clothing of his grandfather.

What happened that night Stefan could never say for sure. When he finally got back to the house, he was so tired that he decided to get some sleep and continue the search in the morning. As he lay down on the bed, he was aware of somebody breathing beside him. Grabbing the lantern, he held it close to the breathing figure. It was his wife Esther!

160

"What is it, Stefan?" she said, sitting up. Then noticing his red feet, she said, "Where have you been?"

Had Stefan been only dreaming and imagined all this? But how did the tomb door get opened? And how did the single footprints get in the snow, and how did the tiny red marks get on Esther's neck?

The figure Esther described, the one she had seen in her dreams, was that of Piztau Lutza, a man who had been dead for over a hundred years.

Notes

THE INFORMATION given in the following notes seems largely self-explanatory, but perhaps some comment on the arrangement is in order. First, I have given my source of the story; in full, I have included the informant's name, his residence, and the date I collected the story, together with the informant's source of the story. Second, there is additional information on the circumstances of the story or its locale which the informant may have given me or which I may have provided. Third, I have mentioned comparisons with ghost stories in other collections or literary uses of certain themes when these have seemed pertinent. Finally, I have listed the motifs present in the story. All of this information is not given for each story; many stories, for example, have only the source and the motifs.

1. *The Phantom Soldier*
   William K. Smith, Clarksburg, 1956.
   The soldier's return, apparently alive, is similar to the return of the RAF officers in a story in *Things That Go Bump in the Night* (pp. 157-58) by Louis C. Jones.
   Motifs: T92.1, the triangle plot and its solutions; E230, return from the dead to inflict punishment.

2. *The Mysterious Horseshoe*
   Bonnie Arnett, Farmington, 1963, as told to her by Mrs. Madeline Buchanan.
   Motifs: T92.1, the triangle plot and its solutions; E426, revenant as object; E421.3, luminous ghosts.

3. *The Domico Family*

John Pienkos, Grant Town, 1959.

Motifs: T92.1, the triangle plot and its solutions; E221.3, dead husband returns to reprove wife's second husband; E231.5, ghost returns to murderer, causes him to confess.

4. *What Price Love?*

Jean West, Fairmont, 1956, as told to her by Mrs. Effie Bunner Hale of Fairmont.

Motifs: T92.1, the triangle plot and its solutions; E422.1.1, headless revenant; E535.2, ghostly wagon.

5. *The Legend of Boiling Springs*

John Parker, Parkersburg, 1958, as told to him by an elderly man who lived near Boiling Springs.

Motifs: T92.1, the triangle plot and its solutions; E402, mysterious ghostlike noises heard.

6. *Hunting Friends*

Alfred De Blassio, Fairmont, 1963, as told to him by Richard Taylor of Preston County.

Although the locale is given as Preston County, the story is probably widely known. In *Things That Go Bump in the Night* (pp. 94-96), Louis C. Jones gives a version of the same tale from the Adirondacks.

Motifs: T92.1, the triangle plot and its solutions; E234.3, return from dead to avenge death (murder).

7. *A Head and a Body*

Robert Leeper, Fairmont, 1954, as told to him by his mother.

According to stories handed down to Mr. Leeper's mother, the scythe murder actually happened, and, supposedly, the ghost cries too. Mt. Harmony is about three and a half miles from Fairmont, just off the road to Morgantown.

The unhappiness of this poor body that could not find its head is very similar to that of "The Headless Hant" in *The Book of Negro Folklore* (pp. 164-65) by Langston Hughes and Arna Bontemps.

Motifs: T92.1, the triangle plot and its solutions; E422.1.1, headless revenant; E412.3, dead without proper funeral rites cannot rest; E419.7, person with missing bodily member cannot rest in grave.

8. *The Telltale Lilac Bush*
Keith Ketchem, 1963, as told to him by Mrs. Sarah Dadisman of Union, Monroe County.
Motifs: E221, dead spouse's malevolent return; E231, return from dead to reveal murder; possibly E631.6, re-incarnation in tree from grave.

9. *The Chain*
Terry Ann Bradley, Mannington, 1963, as told to her by her grandfather.
Motifs: E221, dead spouse's malevolent return; E413, murdered person cannot rest in grave; E402.1.4, invisible ghost jingles chains.

10. *The Face on the Wall*
Frank Savich, Grant Town, 1958, as told to him by his grandfather.
This is somewhat similar to a story in Helen Creighton's *Bluenose Ghosts* (p. 205) in which a dead woman's face appears on the wall of a house she had dreamed of and planned but had not lived to enjoy.
Motifs: E422.1.11.2, revenant as face or head; E322, dead wife's friendly return; E363.1, ghost aids living in emergency.

11. *Bill White's Wife*
Mrs. Josephine Shriver, Littleton, 1950.
Motifs: E221, dead spouse's malevolent return; E402, mysterious ghostlike noises heard.

12. *Uncle Tom Howe*
Harlan M. Bell, Parkersburg, 1957, as told to him by his grandmother.
The story was supposed to have happened in Copen, Braxton County.

Motifs: E221.5, dead wife torments husband who has let her die of neglect; E402.1.3, invisible ghost plays musical instrument.

13. *The Tragedy at the Spring*

Mrs. Josephine Shriver, Littleton, 1950.

Mrs. Shriver says that this is a true happening in Wetzel County, but the places and names are fictitious.

The report that on the anniversary of the killing, the spring water changed to the color of blood is similar to the Life-Token, a track which will fill with blood, set up by the two brothers to notify the other in case of trouble or death, Tale Type 303, II b, or Motif E761.1. This same token, indicating death, occurs in a Hungarian version of "The Two Brothers," which is told in West Virginia.

Motifs: E413, murdered person cannot rest in grave; E402.1.1.3, ghost cries and screams.

14. *The Blue Boy Hotel*

Carol Felosa, Shinnston, 1963, as told to her by Hugh Cox, a 94-year-old Negro who had lived in Shinnston all his life.

Motif: E234.3, return from dead to avenge death (murder).

15. *The Little Rag Doll*

Bonnie Jean Sheets, 1947, as told to her by her mother, who in turn heard it from her mother.

Motifs: E225, ghost of murdered child; E459.3, ghost laid when its wishes are acceded to.

16. *Help*

Terry Ann Bradley, Mannington, 1963, as told to her by her aunt, who heard it from a friend's grandmother.

The incident is supposed to have happened in Wetzel County.

Motifs: E324, dead child's friendly return to parents; E361.1, ghost aids living in emergency; E544.1, ghost leaves object after appearance; a variation of E363.1.1 (a) (Baughman), ghost fetches physician for dying husband.

17. *The Baby in the Fireplace*
   Mrs. Ethel Cunningham, Smithfield, 1948, as told to her by Mrs. Anne Bennett, also of Wetzel County.
   Motifs: E225, ghost of murdered child; E412.3, dead without proper funeral rites cannot rest; E441, ghost laid by reburial.

18. *Rapping on the Door*
   Gary Schoonover, Elkins, 1958, as told to him by Mrs. Roswell Sommerville, who learned the story from Mrs. George Collins, who had lived in the house.
   The story is supposed to have happened about 1935 near the Black Fork section of Cheat River.
   The story of locking a child in the closet for punishment reminds one of a horrifying account given by Helen Creighton in *Bluenose Ghosts* (p. 203). A little Negro slave was hung by her thumbs and locked in a closet, where she died, since the mistress forgot all about her.
   Motifs: E414.1, person killed by accident cannot rest in grave; E402.1.5, invisible ghost makes rapping or knocking noise.

19. *The Boy and the Trumpet*
   Mrs. Ethel Cunningham, Smithfield, 1948.
   Motifs: E422.1.11.4, revenant as skeleton; E554, ghost plays musical instrument.

20. *The Running Child*
   Lana Fridley, Hendricks, 1963, as told to her by relatives.
   Motifs: E225, ghost of murdered child; E413, murdered person cannot rest in grave; E402.1.2, footsteps of invisible ghost heard; E422.1.11.5.1, ineradicable bloodstains in stone or wood floor after bloody tragedy.

21. *The Glass Jug*
   Mrs. Ethel Cunningham, Smithfield, 1948.

167

Motifs: E426, revenant as object; Q211.4, murder of children punished; E234.3, return from dead to avenge death (murder).

22. *Chop Chop*
   Ray Tatterson, Fairmont, 1959, as told to him by Tom Vernon on Bunner's Ridge, an isolated section about ten miles from Fairmont.
   Tom Vernon said it was a true story.
   Fratricide is an old theme in literature, two of the most famous examples being the Cain and Abel story from the Bible and Shakespeare's *Hamlet*.
   Motifs: T92.1, the triangle plot and its solutions; Q211.9, fratricide punished; E220, dead relative's malevolent return; E234.3, return from dead to avenge death (murder); E402, mysterious ghostlike noises heard.

23. *Rose Run*
   Ray Tatterson, Fairmont, 1959, as told to him by Tessie Williams of Bunner's Ridge, who learned the story from her grandfather.
   Motifs: Q211.4, murder of children punished; E230 return from dead to inflict punishment; E426, revenant as object; E631, reincarnation in plant (tree) growing from grave.

24. *The Brother and his Horse*
   Keith Ketchem, 1963, as told to him by Mrs. Sarah Dadisman of Union, Monroe County.
   Motifs: Q211.9, fratricide punished; E220, dead relative's malevolent return; E234.3, return from dead to avenge death (murder); E421.3, luminous ghost; E521.1, ghost of horse.

25. *The Shadow on the Wall*
   Mrs. Ethel Cunningham, Smithfield, 1948.
   Motifs: Q211.9, fratricide punished; E421.4.1 (a) (Baughman), shadow of man on wall.

26. *The Gate*

Ray Tatterson, Fairmont, 1959.

Motif: E402, mysterious ghostlike noises heard.

27. *Shiny Eyes*

Americo Miconi, Carolina, 1961, as told to him by his father.

Motif: E574.5 (h) (Baughman), ghost animal appears as death omen.

28. *The White Horse*

Carmela Mangano, Newell, 1954.

Mason is in southern West Virginia. The incident supposedly took place in 1903.

Vance Randolph reports a story from the Ozarks in *Ozark Superstitions* (p. 381) that seems to involve a similar belief concerning a white horse.

Motif: E574.5 (h) (Baughman), ghost animal appears as death omen.

29. *The White Stallion*

Raymond Stamps, 1958, as told to him by the son of the dying man who was present when the incident occurred.

Motif: E574.5 (h) (Baughman), ghost animal appears as death omen.

30. *White Death*

Frank J. Puskas, Grant Town, 1959.

Motif: E574.5.1 (ha) (Baughman), ghost dog appears as death omen.

31. *A Ride with the Devil*

Robert Lambert, Rivesville, 1955, as told to him by his mother, who heard it from her grandmother.

Motifs: G303.4.4, devil has claws; G303.4.1.6, devil has horns; variation of G303.6.2.8, devil appears to dying man.

32. *A Dream*

   Mrs. Kathryn Heenan, 1950.

   Mrs. Heenan's father's dream of his friend's death is much like the dream of one of the two "felawes" in Chaucer's "Nun's Priest's Tale," in which one dreams of his friend's death. In each instance, on the following day, the dreamer finds out his dream has been fulfilled. Vance Randolph's "Asa Baker's Dream," in *Sticks in the Knapsack* (pp. 125-26), is an Ozark version of this old theme.

   Motif: D1810.8.2.3, murder made known in a dream.

33. *Grandfather's Clock*

   Christina Majastoravich, 1957, as told to her by Lawrence Boggess of Fairmont.

   Motif: D1810.8.2.3, murder made known in a dream.

34. *Death Warning*

   Mrs. Helen M. Norris, formerly of Fairmont, 1948.

   Motif: D1810.8.3.1, warning in dream fulfilled.

35. *The Voice in the Night*

   Mrs. G. G. Tawney, Looneyville, 1959, as told to her by Henry Naylor.

   Motif: E364, dead returns to say farewell.

36. *Vision in a Field*

   Mrs. Gypsy Scott, Smithfield, 1948, as told to her by her mother, who in turn heard it from her grandfather and uncle, the two men who had hoed the cornfield.

   Motif: E574, appearance of ghost serves as death omen.

37. *Captain Copenhaver's Ghost*

   Mrs. Gypsy Scott, Smithfield, 1948.

   Motif: E574, appearance of ghost serves as death omen.

38. *Christmas Tree*

   Mrs. Ethel Cunningham, Smithfield, 1948, as told to her by Dennis Hostuttler of Wetzel County.

   Motifs: E631, reincarnation in plant (tree) growing

from grave; E422.3.1, revenant as small man; E230, return from dead to inflict punishment; E545.2, dead predict death.

39. *Return of the Headless Man*
John M. Cain, Clarksburg, 1959, as told to him by his grandmother.
Motifs: E422.1.1, headless revenant; E411.10, persons who die violent or accidental deaths cannot rest in grave.

40. *The Headless Rider*
Walter Fultz, Clarksburg, 1956, as told to him by his mother, who learned it from his grandmother.
Motifs: E422.1.1, headless revenant; E333.3.1, ghost rides on horseback with rider; E581.2.1, ghost jumps on horse behind man.

41. *The Headless Husband*
Myra Hardy Guin, Fairmont, 1959, as told to her by her teacher, Mrs. Kerns, when she was in the fourth grade.
Motifs: E422.1.1, headless revenant; E411.10, persons who die violent or accidental deaths cannot rest in grave; E544.1.2, ghost leaves a ring with the living.

42. *The Old Well*
Barry Fluharty, Mannington, 1963, as told to him by his uncle.
Motifs: E422.1.1, headless revenant; E421.4, ghost as shadow.

43. *Footsteps on the Walk*
Gene Hickman, Clarksburg, 1958, as told to him by his great-grandmother.
Motifs: E371, return from dead to reveal hidden treasure; E402.1.1, vocal sounds of ghost of human being; E402.1.2, footsteps of invisible ghost heard; E402.1.8, miscellaneous sounds made by ghost of human being.

44. *The Haunted House*
Mrs. Edith Herriman, Fairmont, 1952, as told to her by

R. C. Butler of Morgantown, who learned it from his mother.

A Negro collector from the South told me that he had a number of examples of friendly ghosts that returned first as dogs and then turned into men.

Motifs: E371, return from dead to reveal hidden treasure; E423.1.1, revenant as dog.

45. Aunt Betsy Barr and Her Dog

Mrs. Gypsy Scott, Smithfield, 1948.

Motifs: E371, return from dead to reveal hidden treasure; E341, the grateful dead; E521.2, ghost of dog.

46. The Ghost Girl

H. G. Radebaugh, 1950, as told to him by one of his pupils, Richard Poling, at his school on Mud Lick in Marion County.

Motif: E371, return from dead to reveal hidden treasure.

47. Aunt Bett's Ghost

Mrs. Ethel Cunningham, Smithfield, 1948, as told to her by Virginia Smith, who learned it from her grandfather, Spencer Cunningham.

Motifs: E371, return from dead to reveal hidden treasure; E422.1.11.5.1, ineradicable bloodstain after bloody tragedy.

48. Hickory Nuts

Vernon Giffin, Keyser, 1952, as told to him by Charles W. Cook of near Keyser.

There are many examples of ghosts that explain the reason for their presence when asked in the name of the Creator. In most cases, the ghost is able to rest after this. The white bird, in Vance Randolph's *Ozark Superstitions* (p. 223), was never seen again after being asked what was the matter "in the name of the Father, Son, and Holy Ghost."

Motif: E371, return from dead to reveal hidden treasure.

49. *The Floating Coffin*

Thomas Leeper, Monongah, 1949.

Motifs: E275, ghost haunts place of great accident or misfortune; E538.1, spectral coffin; E386.5, light remark about what person would do if ghost appeared causes ghost to appear.

50. *The Old Burnt House*

Mrs. Josephine Shriver, Littleton, 1950, as told to her by an elderly neighbor, Mr. D—, who lived the greater part of his young days in the house.

Mr. D— said the house was haunted for as long as he could remember.

Motifs: E281, ghost haunts house; E402, mysterious ghostlike noises heard; E422.1.3, revenant with ice-cold hands; E279.3, ghost pulls bedclothing from sleeper; E422.1.11.5.1, ineradicable bloodstain after bloody tragedy; E599.11, locked doors open at touch of ghost; E402.1.6, crash as of breaking glass, though no glass is found broken; E451.8, ghost laid when house it haunts is destroyed or changed.

51. *A Skeleton Hand*

Mrs. Ethel Cunningham, Smithfield, 1948.

Motifs: E281, ghosts haunt house (possibly E281.1, hungry ghosts haunt house seeking food); E422.1.11.3, revenant as hand or hands.

52. *The Upstairs Bedroom*

Mrs. Hazel Booth, 1950, as told to her by Mrs. Eva Finley of Grafton.

Motifs: E281.3, ghost haunts particular room in house; E571, ghostly barber; E544, ghost leaves evidence of his appearance.

53. *Anna Conrad*

Frank Savich, Grant Town, 1960, as told to him by Tony Pasinski, a retired coal miner of Grant Town.

Motifs: E281, ghost haunts house; E544, ghost leaves

evidence of his appearance; E411.1.1, suicide cannot rest in grave; E402.1.1.3, ghost cries and screams.

54. *Wizard's Clipp*

Frank Stemple, 1948, as told to him by Miss Jessie Trotter of Shepherdstown, a retired teacher at Shepherd College.

Miss Trotter said that when she came to Shepherdstown in 1919, there was a case in court regarding the property. Some descendants of Adam Livingston were trying to recover the farm. However, the case was decided in favor of the Catholic Church. There is now on this property a chapel in which services are held once a year, on a certain Thursday in August. The chapel is small, only seating about a dozen people.

Motifs: E412.3, dead without proper funeral rites cannot rest; E230, return from dead to inflict punishment; E412.1, invisible ghost; E443.2.1, ghost laid by saying masses.

55. *Vinegar Hill*

Aaron Miller, 1959, as told to him by Mrs. Marguerite Vincent of Benton's Ferry.

Motifs: E411.10, persons who die violent or accidental deaths cannot rest in grave; E587, ghosts walk at certain times; E599.10, playful revenant.

56. *The Living Corpse*

Gene Hickman, Clarksburg, 1958.

Mr. Hickman grew up in Lost Creek.

Motifs: E411.10, persons who die violent or accidental deaths cannot rest in grave; E275, ghost haunts place of great accident or misfortune; E230, return of dead to inflict punishment.

57. *Old Gopher*

Carol Felosa, Shinnston, 1963, as told to her by Mrs. Lane of Shinnston, who learned it from her father-in-law about 1890.

Motifs: E234.3, return from dead to avenge death

(murder); E272.3, ghost frightens people off bridge into stream; E422.1.1.4, headless ghost carries head under arm; E423.1.8, revenant as cow.

58. *The Ghost of Gamble's Run*
    Terry Ann Bradley, Mannington, 1963, as told to her by residents of Wetzel County.
    Motif: E234.3, return from dead to avenge death (murder).

59. *The Tombstone*
    Herschel Conoway, Fairmont, 1959, as told to him by his grandfather, who heard the story from the slaveowner's son.
    Motifs: E234.3, return from dead to avenge death (murder); E402, mysterious ghostlike noises heard; E413, murdered person cannot rest in grave.

60. *How Kettle Run Was Named*
    Aaron Miller, 1959, as told to him by Mrs. Marguerite Vincent of Benton's Ferry.
    Motifs: E413, murdered person cannot rest in grave; E419.7, person with missing bodily member cannot rest in grave.

61. *The Cruel Slave Master*
    C. T. Gillette, Fairmont, 1955, as told to him by Thomas Jackson, an old Negro of Valley Falls.
    Motif: E234.3, return from dead to avenge death (murder).

62. *The Unusual Saddle*
    Lawrence Himes, Jr., Grafton, 1963, as told to him by Robert Mechem of Berkeley Springs.
    Motif: E419.7, person with missing bodily member cannot rest in grave.

63. *A Ball of Fire*
    Joel K. Zoeffel, 1957, as told to him by William Wease of Glenville.

I have a second version of this story written by Robert Tuttle in 1956. In it the ghost tells the whole story to the judge, and the guilty man is convicted. Otherwise the two versions are essentially the same. Mr. Tuttle said his version was current in Gilmer County.

Vance Randolph also reports several ghosts of murdered peddlers.

Motifs: E334.3.5 (e) (Baughman) ghost of murdered peddler seen near burial spot; E234.3, return from dead to avenge death (murder); E413, murdered person cannot rest in grave; variation of E422.1.1.2, revenant with ball of fire in place of head.

64. *The Murdered Merchant's Ghost*

Mrs. Gertrude Newlon, 1948, as told to her by her father of Wirt County.

This story is the only example I have in which what is apparently the same ghost appears in five or more different forms.

Motifs: E334.3.5 (e) (Baughman), ghost of murdered peddler seen near burial spot; E413, murdered person cannot rest in grave; E422.1.1, headless revenant; E423, revenant in animal form.

65. *Strange Noises*

Franklin D. Shaffer, Thomas, 1956, as told to him by his mother, who in turn heard it from her mother, who learned it from her brother.

This is supposed actually to have happened in Grant County. When Mr. Shaffer's great-uncle stayed at the inn two years later, he and his relatives were convinced that the place was haunted.

The account of the stabbing and dragging may have taken place, but the story seems to be a version of part of Chaucer's "Nun's Priest's Tale," retold from Cicero or Valerius Maximus. This would make the story at least 2,000 years old.

Motifs: D1812.4, future revealed by presentiment; E334.2.1, ghost of murdered person haunts burial spot;

E337.1.1, murder sounds heard just as they must have happened at the time of death.

66. *The Tin Cup*
Terry Ann Bradley, Mannington, 1963, as told to her by her father, who heard it from oldtimers who worked in Calhoun County many years ago.
Motifs: variation of E334.3.5 (e) (Baughman), ghost of murdered peddler seen near burial spot; E275, ghost haunts place of great accident or misfortune; E421.1.3, ghost visible to dogs alone.

67. *Big John's Ghost*
Jim Cliburn, Grant Town, 1957, as told to him by his grandfather.
Big John's story is reminiscent of some of the accounts recorded in Newbell N. Puckett's *Folk Beliefs of the Southern Negro* (p. 127): "In another case a murderer chopped a man's head off; to his everlasting horror the head began to talk to him. Another man was decapitated in a railroad wreck. His headless body walked up and down the track asking if anyone was hurt."
Motifs: E334.4.1 (a) (Baughman), persons killed in mine accidents haunt place of death; E422.1.1.4, headless ghost carries head under arm.

68. *The Pointing Finger*
Frank J. Puskas, Grant Town, 1959, as told to him by his father, who has worked in the Grant Town mine for years.
Motif: E422.1.11.3, ghost as hand or hands.

69. *The Old Horse*
Frank J. Puskas, Grant Town, 1959, as told to him by his father.
"The Old Horse" is not a ghost story, as I see it, and was probably not intended to be. It is a kind of miracle, like Balaam's ass. Vance Randolph has a short tale of a talking turtle, in his *The Talking Turtle and Other Stories,*

that limits his talk to two sessions—with not too large a vocabulary—but he certainly accomplishes things nevertheless. The talking mule seems to be fairly common in Negro folktales, with such examples as "Dat Mule is Talkin'" in *A Treasury of American Folk Humor,* edited by James N. Tidwell, "Old Boss, John, and the Mule" in *Terrapin's Pot of Sense* by Harold Courlander, and "The Talking Mule" in *Negro Folktales in Michigan* by Richard M. Dorson. All of these are humorous examples of talking animals, but in "The Old Horse" the situation is serious.

Motif: B210, speaking animals.

70. *Section South Main*
Frank J. Puskas, Grant Town, 1959, as told to him by his father.
Motif: E334.4.1 (a) (Baughman), persons killed in mine accidents haunt place of death.

71. *The Blue Flame*
Patricia Reho, 1963, as told to her by her grandfather.
The blue light is commonly associated with ghosts and the supernatural. In Shakespeare's *Richard III* (V, iii), for example, the lights burn blue after the appearance of the ghosts on the night before the battle of Bosworth Field. In *Ozark Superstitions* (p. 235), Vance Randolph mentions a bluish light seen near a cemetery.
Motifs: E334.4.1 (a) (Baughman), persons killed in mine accidents haunt place of death; E336.1 (Baughman), helpful mine ghosts; E530.1, ghostlike lights.

72. *Big Max*
Carl McKinney, Fairmont, 1959.
Motifs: E334.4.1 (a) (Baughman), persons killed in mine accidents haunt place of death; E363, return of dead to help the living.

73. *The Ghost of Jeremy Walker*
John Kaznoski, Barrackville, 1961, as told to him by his uncle.

Motif: E336.1.2.3 (bc) (Baughman), ghost of miner helps friend load mine car.

74. *Post Inspection*
Walter C. Sibley, 1958, as told to him by Mr. Barron, who still worked in the Idamay mine at the time.
Motif: E354 (Baughman), dead returns to complete task.

75. *The First Husband of Mrs. James*
John Pienkos, Grant Town, 1960, as told to him by Mrs. Welch, a neighbor.
Motif: E336.1.2.5 (Baughman), ghost warns miner of danger.

76. *Possessed*
Valentino Zabolotny, 1954, as told to him by Mrs. Rose Rote of Fairmont, who knew of the incident.
The old Gaston mine, no longer in existence, was on Highway 73, about two miles from Fairmont and this side of Watson. The Gaston Gas and Coal Company (1875-1925) had the first mine explosion in the United States in 1880.
I have several other stories of possession, all of Italian origin, I believe.
Motifs: variation of E725.2, ghost possesses girl and she speaks in dialect unknown to her; E412.3, dead without proper funeral rites cannot rest; E443.2.1, ghost laid by saying masses.

77. *The Body under the Train*
Charles G. Wilburn, Fairmont, 1956, as told to him by his grandfather in Preston County.
Motifs: E334.2.2, ghost of person killed in accident seen at death or burial spot; E422.1.1, headless revenant.

78. *Boardtree Tunnel*
Mrs. Josephine Shriver, Littleton, 1950, as told to her by a neighbor of Packie Henderick.
Boardtree Tunnel is on the Baltimore and Ohio railroad

between Fairmont and Wheeling, near the towns of Little-ton and Boardtree. About 2,400 feet long, it was started in 1852 and completed in 1858.

Motifs: E599.10, playful revenant; E334.2.2, ghost of person killed in accident seen at death of burial spot.

79. *The Headless Man*

Gary Schoonover, Elkins, 1958, as told to him by Idris Adams of Fairmont, who learned it from her father, Joe Board.

Motifs: E422.1.1, headless revenant; E334.2.2, ghost of person killed in accident seen at death or burial spot.

80. *The Phantom Wreck*

Richard Baumgardner, 1963, as told to him by Mike More of Rowlesburg.

In *Things That Go Bump in the Night,* Louis C. Jones mentions a phantom of the Lincoln funeral train that appears once a year. B. A. Botkin in his *Treasury of American Folklore* gives an account of "The Phantom Train of Marshall Pass," which includes a phantom wreck. In this story the engineer sees what he thinks is another train coming up behind him; he races ahead, only to see the other train turn off the track and wreck, and the whole thing proves illusory.

Motifs: E535.4.3 (Baughman), phantom train reenacts wreck; E337.2, reenactment of tragedy seen.

81. *The Tortured Sparrow*

Anonymous, about 1950.

Until about 1863, Fairmont was called Middletown—between Morgantown and Clarksburg—and as late as 1885, East Fairmont was known as Palatine.

This story seems to be related to the "plucked gorby" stories told in the Northeast.

Motif: E524, ghost of bird.

82. *The Canary*

Frank J. Puskas, Grant Town, 1959, as told to him by his father.

Because of their sensitivity to its fumes, canaries were often used in coal mines to detect the presence of gas.

Motifs: E524, ghost of bird; E275, ghost haunts place of great accident or misfortune; E363.2, ghost returns to protect the living.

83. *The Cat*

Mrs. G. G. Tawney, Looneyville, 1959, as told to her by Henry Naylor.

Ghost cats are not very common. In one story I have collected, a railroadman kills a cat for no reason at all, and afterward he sees the cat staring at him from a certain train as it passes by. Helen Creighton, in *Bluenose Ghosts* (p. 165), has a ghost kitten playing with a ball of yarn.

Motifs: E521.3, ghost of cat; E337, ghost reenacts scene from own lifetime; E402, mysterious ghostlike noises heard.

84. *The Bench-Legged Dog*

Thomas Leeper, Monongah, 1949, as told to him by his father, Henry P. Leeper, a Methodist preacher, who ministered in Monongalia, Preston, and Tucker counties.

The run back of Barrackville referred to in this story was evidently Finch's Run. There is a Strait's Run several miles away, and it may have been along here that Henry Leeper saw the "bench-legged dog on the flat rock." At one time the J. O. Watson home at Fort Hill was owned by a Mr. Straight, so that this may have been the locality where the dog bit the child and was later killed and cut up by the drunken men. Fort Hill is about half a mile off the road to Wheeling, a mile or two from Barrackville, and six or seven miles from Fairmont. This particular spot is comparatively level, although there are hills all around it.

Helen Creighton, Louis C. Jones, George Korson, and Vance Randolph all report tales of ghost dogs, some of them headless, and some invisible or disappearing.

Motifs: E521.2, ghost of dog; E235, return from dead to punish indignities to corpse or ghost; E275, ghost haunts place of great accident or misfortune.

85. *The White Wolf*
    Lester Tinnell, 1954.
    French Creek is a small town in the central part of the state. Although the town itself is comparatively level, it is surrounded by hills.
    Motifs: E423.2.7, revenant as wolf; E230, return from dead to inflict punishment.

86. *The Phantom Dog*
    Roy A. West, French Creek, 1952.
    Motifs: E521.2, ghost of dog; E421.1.1, ghost visible to one person alone.

87. *The Old Sow*
    Roy A. West, French Creek, 1952.
    Motifs: E423.1.5, revenant as swine; E402, mysterious ghostlike noises heard; E421.1, invisible ghost.

88. *The Junkman's Horse*
    Harry Hobbs, Monongah, 1961.
    Motifs: E521.1, ghost of horse; E230, return from dead to inflict punishment; E234.3, return from dead to avenge death (murder); E235, return from dead to punish indignities to corpse.

89. *Jack*
    John Yokay, Carolina, 1959, as told to him by Joseph Schutz, an elderly boarder at his grandmother's.
    Mr. Schutz said he was in the mines when this incident happened.
    Motifs: E521.1, ghost of horse; E340, return from dead to repay obligation; E363.2, ghost returns to protect the living.

90. *The Strange Chicken*
    John Kaznoski, Barrackville, 1961, as told to him by his grandfather.
    Motifs: E613, reincarnation as bird; B211.3.2.1, speaking chicken.

91. *A Loyal Dog*
    Harry Hobbs, Monongah, 1961, as told to him by a neighbor.
    Motifs: E521.2, ghost of dog; E363.2, ghost returns to protect the living; E544, ghost leaves evidence of his appearance.

92. *The White Thing*
    Thomas A. Burford, Charleston, 1954.
    Mr. Burford says this is a common tale in Kanawha County.
    "Old Horny," in Vance Randolph's *The Talking Turtle and Other Stories* (pp. 169-70), might be classed as a creature story. Most such stories, however, are more terrifying and less understandable.
    Motif: E423, revenant in animal form. It is perhaps questionable whether these stories fall within any present classification as the creatures do not seem to be revenants, but rather malevolent supernatural manifestations of another order.

93. *The Strange Creature*
    Michael O'Dell, Rivesville, 1958.
    Mr. O'Dell says this is a true story.
    Motif: E423, revenant in animal form.

94. *Shortcut*
    Katherine Kozul, Fairmont, 1963, as told to her by her father.
    Motif: E423, revenant in animal form.

95. *The White Figure*
    Neva Jean Duvall. Philippi, 1955, as told to her by her aunt of Lambert's Run.
    Motif: E423, revenant in animal form.

96. *Seven Bones*
    Anna Krajnak, Fairmont, 1948, as told to her by her mother.

183

Anton Dvorak's *The Spectre's Bride,* a dramatic cantata, is the best artistic treatment of this tale.

Tale Type 365, the dead bridegroom carries off his bride (Lenore).

Motifs: E215, the dead rider (Lenore); E266, dead carry off living; E34.8, ghost cannot pass cross or prayer book; E452, ghost laid at cockcrow.

97. *The Corpse That Wouldn't Stay Buried*

Mrs. Anne Conley, Fairmont, 1953, as told to her in Polish by her uncle, John Novak.

An amusing parallel to this story of a corpse who would not remain decently in his grave is found in "Daid Aaron," in Langston Hughes and Arna Bontemps' *The Book of Negro Folklore* (pp. 175-78). In this story, Aaron Kelly walks into the wake that is being held for him just as his widow is saying, "Ah hopes 'e gone whuh ah spec's 'e ain't!" Aaron doesn't feel dead and says he isn't going to be buried again until he does. Everything gets to be in a bad way because the insurance people won't pay, the widow can't pay for the coffin, the undertaker is about to reclaim the coffin, and so on. The widow explains all this to Aaron, but Aaron still refuses to be buried again. Finally the best fiddler in town comes to court the widow, but there is little they can do about getting married with Aaron sitting warming his feet and hands at the fire. Aaron says that since everyone is so dismal, the fiddler should play some dancing music. Aaron dances faster and faster until one of his bones after another falls to the floor, but his head keeps on dancing. The fiddler is so shocked by this that he runs off and never comes back, and the widow never does get married. Aaron is buried for the second time with his bones all mixed up so that he cannot very well get himself back together, and this time he never returns.

Motifs: E410, the unquiet grave; E459.3, ghost laid when its wishes are acceded to.

98. *Draga's Return*

Homer Delovich, Monongah, 1957, as told to him by his grandfather.

This Yugoslavian tale seems to be a variation of the vampire theme in that driving a stake through the heart was believed to be a way to kill a vampire. Here the heart is not specifically mentioned.

Motifs: E436.2, cats crossing one's path a sign of ghosts (possibly); E422.1.3, revenant with ice-cold hands; E422.1.4, revenant with cold lips; E471, ghost kisses living person; E442, ghost laid by piercing grave (corpse) with stake.

99. *The Old Crossroads*

Gloria Guido Forte, 1954, as told to her by her father of Grant Town, who had heard his father tell it in Italy.

Motifs: E234.3, return from dead to avenge death (murder); E423.7, revenant as fly; E726, soul enters body and animates it.

100. *Footprints in the Snow*

Frank J. Puskas, Grant Town, 1959, as told to him by his father.

Motif: E251, vampire.

Bibliography

Aarne, Antti, and Thompson, Stith. *The Types of the Folk-Tale.* Folklore Fellows Communications, Vol. XXV, No. 74. Helsinki, 1928.

Baughman, Ernest W. "A Comparative Study of the Folktales of England and North America." 3 vols. Unpublished Ph.D. Dissertation, Indiana University, 1953.

Beardsley, Richard K., and Hankey, Rosalie. "A History of the Vanishing Hitchhiker." *California Folklore Quarterly,* II (January 1943), 13-44.

—————————. "The Vanishing Hitchhiker." *California Folklore Quarterly,* I (October 1942), 303-35.

Beck, Horace P. *The Folklore of Maine.* New York, Lippincott, 1957.

Botkin, B. A. (ed.) *A Treasury of American Folklore.* New York, Crown, 1944.

—————————. *A Treasury of Southern Folklore.* New York, Crown, 1949.

Cohen, Bernard, and Ehrenpreis, Irvin. "Tales from Indiana University Students." *Hoosier Folklore,* VI (June 1947), 57-65.

Courlander, Harold. *Terrapin's Pot of Sense.* New York, Holt, 1957.

Creighton, Helen. *Bluenose Ghosts.* Toronto, Ryerson, 1957.

Foster, James R. (ed.) *Lovers, Mates, and Strange Bedfellows.* New York, Harper, 1960.

Gardner, Emelyn E. *Folklore from the Schoharie Hills of New York.* Ann Arbor, Michigan, 1937.

187

Harden, John. *Tar Heel Ghosts.* Chapel Hill, North Carolina, 1954.

Hughes, Langston, and Bontemps, Arna. *The Book of Negro Folklore.* New York, Dodd, Mead, 1958.

Hyatt, Harry M. *Folk-Lore from Adams County, Illinois.* New York, Alma Eagan Hyatt Foundation, 1935.

Jones, Louis C. "Hitchhiking Ghosts in New York." *California Folklore Quarterly,* III (October 1944), 284-92.

——————. *Spooks of the Valley.* Boston, Houghton Mifflin, 1948.

——————. *Things That Go Bump in the Night.* New York, Hill and Wang, 1959.

Korson, George. *Black Rock: Mining Folklore of the Pennsylvania Dutch.* Baltimore, Johns Hopkins, 1960.

Musick, Ruth Ann. *Ballads, Folk-songs and Folk-tales from West Virginia.* Morgantown: West Virginia University Library, 1960.

——————. "Iowa Student Tales." *Hoosier Folklore,* V (September 1946), 103-10.

——————. "Omens and Tokens of West Virginia." *Midwest Folklore,* II (Winter 1952-1953), 263-67.

——————. "The Murdered Pedlar in West Virginia." *Midwest Folklore,* XI (Winter 1961-1962), 247-55.

——————. "The Old Folks Say." Column in Fairmont *Times-West Virginian,* 1948-1954.

——————. "West Virginia Folklore." *Hoosier Folklore,* VII (March 1948), 1-14.

——————. "West Virginia Ghost Stories." *Midwest Folklore,* VIII (Spring 1958), 21-28.

Puckett, Newbell N. *Folk Beliefs of the Southern Negro.* Chapel Hill, North Carolina, 1926.

Randolph, Vance. *Ozark Superstitions.* New York, Columbia, 1947.

——————. *Sticks in the Knapsack.* New York, Columbia, 1958.

——————. *The Devil's Pretty Daughter.* New York, Columbia, 1955.

——————. *The Talking Turtle.* New York, Columbia, 1957.

——————. *Who Blowed Up the Church House?* New York, Columbia, 1952.

Seymour, St. John D., and Neligan, Harry L. *True Irish Ghost Stories*. Dublin, Hodges, Figgis, 1914.

Thompson, Stith. *Motif-Index of Folk Literature*, 6 vols. Indiana University Studies, Bloomington, 1931-1936.

————————. *Motif-Index of Folk Literature*, New enl. and rev. ed. 6 vols. Bloomington, Indiana, 1955-1958.

————————. *The Folktale*. New York, Dryden Press, 1946.

Tidwell, James N. (ed.) *A Treasury of American Folk Humor*. New York, Crown, 1956.

West Virginia Folklore. Ghost story issues: III (Fall 1952); V (Fall 1954); VII (Fall 1956); VIII (Summer 1958). Mining issues: X (Fall 1959); X (Winter 1959-60); XIII (Fall 1963).